BRIAN KAVANAGH

A CANTERBURY

A BELINDA LAWRENCE MYSTERY

CRIME

VIVID
PUBLISHING

Copyright © 2013 Brian Kavanagh

Published by Vivid Publishing
A division of the Fontaine Publishing Group
P.O. Box 948 Fremantle
Western Australia 6959
www.vividpublishing.com.au

National Library of Australia Cataloguing-in-Publication data:
Author: Kavanagh, Brian, 1935-, author.
Title: A Canterbury crime / Brian Kavanagh.
ISBN: 9781922204516 (paperback)
Series: Belinda Lawrence mystery.
Dewey Number: A823.4

To discover more Brian Kavanagh books, to contact the author, please visit www.vividpublishing.com.au/briankavanagh for further information.

To my brother, Gerald. Relationships may fail and friends come and go, but brothers are forever.

Brian Kavanagh has many years' experience in the Australian Film Industry in areas of production, direction, editing and writing. His editing credits include *The Chant Of Jimmie Blacksmith, Odd Angry Shot, The Devil's Playground, Long Weekend, Sex Is A Four-Letter Word* and the recent comedy, *Dags*. He received a Lifetime Achievement Award from the Australian Film Editors Guild and an Australian Film Institute award for Best Editing for *Frog Dreaming*. His first feature film which he produced and directed, *A City's Child*, won an AFI award for actress Monica Maughan and was screened at the London Film Festival as well as Edinburgh, Montreal, Chicago and Adelaide, where it won the Gold Southern Cross Advertiser Award for Best Australian Film.

A Canterbury Crime

Canterbury

Canterbury in South East England is in the County of Kent and roughly sixty miles from London. It began as an Iron Age settlement and when the Romans invaded they rebuilt the Celtic settlement and named it Durovernum Cantiacorum.

After the Romans left Britain, the Pope in 597 AD ordered St Augustine and his fellow monks to convert the Saxons. They built an abbey outside the walls of the town. Canterbury was created the seat of the first archbishop.

The town thrived but endured harsh times when the Danes invaded England. The early cathedral was burned and rebuilt several times.

After the murder of Thomas Becket on 26th December 1170, Canterbury became famed throughout Europe and the Canterbury Tales of Chaucer recounts the stories told by a fictional group of pilgrims.

The present-day cathedral was begun under Archbishop Lanfranc, the first Norman archbishop and built between 1070 and 1180 and from 1379 to 1503. The east chapel is called the Corona or Becket's Crown; Trinity Chapel, which held the shrine of St Thomas until 1538, when Henry VIII ordered it destroyed. In the north western transept a memorial Cross commemorates the exact site of Thomas Becket's murder.

During World War II the cathedral was the target of harsh German bombing raids. While the cathedral itself received no direct hit, bombs destroyed the library and numerous other adjacent buildings and 115 people were killed.

The city of Canterbury is of interest, with a 14th-century Westgate and remains of the old city walls; St Martin's Church, created before St Augustine's arrival; the long-standing pilgrims' hostel called the Hospital of St Thomas and quite a few old inns. Christopher Marlowe was born in Canterbury and educated at King's School there before going to Cambridge.

Chaucer wrote of the pilgrims in his day and the town still attracts tourists – as well as pilgrims to honour St Thomas Becket.

Chapter One

"Blood. She said there was blood on his head."

Hazel Whitby took a healthy gulp of gin. She and Belinda Lawrence were relaxing in their hotel lounge after a busy and intriguing first day making a tentative start on cataloguing the vast, seemingly endless, number of objects at the Manor House. Faintly in the background they could hear the boys' choir, cloistered in the Cathedral, their blameless voices proclaiming an Advent Carol service.

"But the doctor said it was a heart attack," said Hazel cynically. "First time I've heard of a heart attack giving you a bloody head."

Belinda looked thoughtful as she contemplated what had happened in the past two days and the beginnings of a mystery surrounding the death of Professor de Gray.

Christmas had come to Canterbury and so had Belinda and Hazel. They had left Bath in Somerset for Kent the day before and on arrival in Canterbury later that evening had parked Hazel's Mercedes in the hoped for safety of a nearby car-park. The two women then made their way through the Christmas throng of excited children, weary mothers and jubilant tourists to Burgate and their hotel near Christchurch Gate, the entrance to the Cathedral grounds. Brightly lit shop interiors accentuated the darkness of the streets, offering warmth and comfort in exchange for the purchase of glittering and enticing riches. Christmas Carols assaulted their ears along with the excited chatter of the children, "Ho, Ho, Ho" from numerous Santas and the chimes of the bells from the nearby Cathedral. Fairy lights flickered in the chill dark of the early evening and added to the festive atmosphere.

They wearily climbed the steps to the hotel reception desk in silence. Actually they had been silent for the last two hours, both women taking pleasure in what could only be called a fit of piqué. Belinda had wanted to visit Chawton and Jane Austen's House on the way to Canterbury and was annoyed when they arrived to find that the Museum had just closed for the day. This she blamed on Hazel, who had been late arriving to collect her from her cottage in Milford, so the tension between the two women had been building all afternoon.

Belinda's irritation would have increased if she'd known that Hazel had purposely been late, as she had no intention of trudging around a stuffy museum looking at facsimiles of nineteenth century letters, decaying copies of books and twee lace mittens, and only wanted to get to Canterbury as quickly as possible, hopefully to kick off her shoes, have a drink and relax before the evening meal. After all they were starting work at the Manor House early the next day and from then on there wouldn't be much time to relax.

Much of Hazel's annoyance came from her doctor's orders to stop smoking. *What did he mean a woman of my age? Forty, well all right, fifty. Well all right, fifty-plus if you're going to be pedantic.* So far, she had been successful in following his orders, but at the expense of what little good-will she normally felt for her fellow man.

The way to their hotel rooms had led them on a path pilgrims to Canterbury trod centuries ago, to follow meandering corridors encircled by ancient tiled rooftops, over slanting floors, through low doorways, under a heavy beamed ceiling, past a guest lounge and a spectacular view of the great Cathedral, so close that Belinda felt she could almost reach out and touch it. Now, lit as it was, the medieval house of worship became a golden beacon of light amidst the sinewy fingers of skeletal winter trees and the shimmering white illuminated Christmas tree, by the South-West entrance, an invitation to worship and peace on earth.

Its peaceful expectations seemed to have infected both women and, as soon as they had explored their rooms, unpacked and freshened up, the daftness of their spat passed off and they headed to the lounge, both chuckling over some curious item they'd found in a tourist brochure.

Hazel had just taken her first sip of the longed for refreshing drink when the chimes of Belinda's mobile phone ruined the calm of the lounge.

"Mark?" Belinda rose and continued her conversation as she stood and looked out at the Cathedral.

Hazel watched her young friend. Tall, slim, dark hair, blue eyes. Young? How old was Belinda now? Late twenties? How many years had they known each other? Four years? Five? Probably four since the young Australian had inherited the cottage in the tiny village of Milford on the outskirts of Bath. Since then she had become an enthusiastic partner in Hazel's antique business, which had grown in leaps and bounds. Hazel envied her partner's relaxed attitude to life that came from an Australian upbringing and the informal lifestyle there. The restricted surroundings of England had not limited her nature and her inborn vivacity added to her natural beauty. Belinda had been a willing learner and Hazel relied on her keenness, skills and understanding as she initiated the younger woman into the world of antiques.

The older woman glanced at the hand that held her glass.

"Antique," she muttered. *Why was it that a woman's hands revealed her age no matter how much make-up, botox and surgery, not to mention money, one spent keeping the rest supple and, if not young, at least youthful – if one was prepared to suspend disbelief?* She'd read of some new treatment that was supposed to give you the hands of a teenager but from the 'before and after' photographs she saw very little difference. They were still claws. Hazel sighed, not for the first time at the ravages of age. They said the fifties were the new thirties. The fifty-year old, who made that specious claim, she decided, hadn't tried getting out of a chair quickly, or elegantly. Or climbed a set of stairs without a fuselage of crackles and creaks as primordial bones cried out in protest.

A laugh from Belinda brought her back from such distressing facts and she sipped her gin thoughtfully. Mark Sallinger. Mark was Belinda's English, more-or-less boyfriend, dark good looks, wealthy and keen to marry, but Belinda had so far declined his offers.

They had been lovers for some years and now he had a successful real estate business handling top of the range country estates, Mark urged Belinda to agree to his proposal. Belinda hesitated. She loved Mark fervently but she wanted to be sure. There was Brad, an Australian boyfriend, for whom she still felt something. Also, Belinda had confided in Hazel that she was a little in awe of Mark's family: his recently deceased father had had a title and she sometimes felt a little out of her depth with his mother who, although charming on the surface, sometimes gave the impression that she wasn't impressed with her son's infatuation with 'someone from the colonies'.

Hazel gave a self-satisfied smile. At least she didn't have to worry about marriage. She'd tried that, only to have her husband run off with some giddy, gauche teenager who, Hazel had been delighted to hear, had recently dumped him and married a French millionaire. The settlement she had on her own divorce had helped set her up with her string of antique shops and allowed her the luxury of a string of gentlemen friends – with strictly no strings attached, so that anyone meeting Hazel Whitby for the first time would see an attractive mature woman, still with a strong sexual allure, an appetite for the better things in life and a determination to practise them with every intention of living to tell the tale.

Belinda snapped the phone shut and stood before Hazel.

"Mark will be here in a day or so, so we can spend Christmas here. I'm hungry. Shall we go into dinner and you can tell me the real reason we're in Canterbury and what to expect tomorrow when we go to the Manor House."

At nine o'clock the next morning Belinda waited impatiently at the foot of the hotel steps and watched the morning activities in Buttermarket as locals went about their business, French students queued to enter the Cathedral grounds and a tourist group slavishly followed their jaded guide. The crisp morning air was exhilarating and the unexpected blue sky promised a sunny, if cold, day. Belinda squeezed her hands tight, protected as they were in thick woollen gloves. Prepared for the cold she was dressed in wool trousers, alpaca sweater and a warm, check patterned jacket.

Belinda had long wanted to visit Canterbury with its Roman origins and fascinating history. Damaged during World War II, the bombing raids had exposed numerous Roman baths, streets, walls and theatres. And there had been the shrine of St Thomas Becket, who was murdered in the cathedral, a highlight of pilgrimages Chaucer wrote about.

So much history, thought Belinda excitedly, who was eager to explore the old walled town.

The prospect of Christmas in Canterbury with Mark was even more pleasing, and one of the many perquisites of working with Hazel was the opportunity to travel around England dealing with antiques. It seemed that this assignment was to be no different.

She heard footsteps behind her, turned to greet Hazel and bit back a smile as the older woman stepped into the sunlight. Hazel had gone retro, in this case, retro 1940s and in her black formfitting dress, overcoat with padded shoulders, and a black turban encasing her head, she reminded Belinda of a film star about to take the oath in a dramatic nineteen-forties courtroom drama. Belinda did enjoy Hazel's company and knew that the sometimes autocratic manner she adopted was pure theatre and often wondered why Hazel hadn't considered the possibility that her true milieu was the stage.

Having located their car and eventually finding their way out of the old city, they drove east along Longport and past the ruins of St Augustine's Abbey. Belinda glanced at the sheaf of papers Hazel had given her.

"From what you said last night, this professor died about six months ago?"

"Professor Walter de Gray," said Hazel, as she tooted a fractious car horn at an innocent cyclist, who was doing no harm to any man. "Yes. A history professor specializing in medieval history, in particular Church law."

As they continued, Belinda noted a sign leading to 'St Martin's Church, A World Heritage Site' and filed that exciting detail away for a future visit. She glanced down at the information sheet she held.

"We turn right at the next corner."

This led them into Spring Lane and they proceeded past a cluster of commuter houses and eventually into open fields. At a point where the main road turned to the left, a long laneway stretched ahead leading to a copse of Oak trees. Hazel drove towards it.

"This looks like the place," she muttered.

Passing through the trees they came to a dejected overgrown garden with a circular driveway, a dry fountain in the centre and a house beyond. Belinda's first glimpse of the two storey imposing tiled and timbered bulk, hidden away forlorn and unwelcoming, took her breath away.

The jettied Manor House, the upper storey overhanging the floor below, stood as it had for over four hundred years in the midst of the copse shielded from the prying eyes and the passing years. The Tudor building, with a porch concealing the front door as though to evaluate any interloper seeking admittance, gave the impression that it was prepared to concede defeat and sink into the ground, its wooden structure weary of the centuries past and now seeking respite.

The two women approached the door in the porch.

"It's magnificent, but rather run down," said Belinda as she looked at the façade.

Hazel grinned.

"But my instinct tells me it's an Aladdin's Cave," she said, employing the hefty doorknocker shaped in the form of a dolphin, thereby giving enthusiastic notice of her arrival.

As she waited impatiently she adjusted her turban, tucked a wayward lock of blonde hair back into its top-security prison. Blonde hair she reminded herself, that had required her to sit in the torturous stylist's chair for a solid eight hours and then had made a serious assault on her credit card.

The ancient door was opened by a hearty woman in her sixties, her robust figure encased in a violent floral smock, grey hair shaped to a bun on the top of her head, below which were two prominent eyes full of curiosity. The woman choked back a chuckle at the sight of Joan Crawford standing on the door step. *Mildred Pearce, wasn't it?*

Hazel, sensing the woman's amusement at her expense, drew herself to her full height and eyed the subordinate with distaste.

"I'm Mrs Hazel Whitby. I have an appointment with Miss Muriel Mowbray."

The woman smiled and ushered them into a small entrance hall, the oak panelled walls of which were covered with a plethora of old military weapons and maces.

"Of course. I'll take you up to the solar. If you'll kindly wait there I'll tell Miss Muriel, if I can find her that is. She's here I know but with so many rooms she could be anywhere. I know she is expecting you. I'm the house keeper, Mrs Day."

Hazel sniffed in a manner to indicate that the woman could have been named Boudicca for all she cared. Mrs Day guided them up an oak doglegged staircase into a large room heavily endowed with furniture from a mixture of periods, some Victorian, some Georgian and some that appeared to be even earlier.

Mrs Day smiled to herself once more as she watched Hazel, full of her own self- importance, stride into the room.

"Make yourselves comfortable and I'll just go and get Miss Muriel."

She bustled off and the two women took in their surroundings.

"This is amazing," said Belinda, as she wandered about taking in the contents of the room.

Hazel ran a skilled eye over a Jacobean chair.

"Hmmm, and I suspect there's more to come."

The high timbered arched roof looked down on a comfortable room. A large stone fireplace, set now for a fire but unlit, dominated the space. The walls were bare apart from a worn tapestry above the fireplace, a few framed watercolours nearby and some brass rubbings. One wall had a book case filled to over flowing with books of all kind while an 18th Century walnut bureau bookcase hid its contents from view behind closed doors. A Persian rug attempted to conceal the worn wooden floor but, defeated, retired to the centre of the room. High arched windows let pale winter light into the room and below them stood a small table and chairs, presumably for the taking of meals judging by the place mats and crystal cruet set. Other small tables scattered throughout the room held silver plates, jugs, candlesticks and various pottery objects.

Belinda inspected a porcelain vase.

"What did the housekeeper call this room? Solar?"

"An old fashioned name for drawing room. In these houses the main room was the Great Hall, where the whole household mucked in and ate meals and lived, more or less, cheek by jowl. Messy business I imagine," said Hazel as she looked at the hallmark on a silver bowl. "Eventually the owner and his family got fed up with this arrangement and wanted some privacy, so the solar was created where they could get away from the goings-on in the Great Hall."

"Mrs Whitby?"

Hazel almost dropped the bowl and Belinda jumped, as they had not heard the woman enter. She seemed to have materialized out of nowhere. She took a step closer.

"I'm Muriel Mowbray. Thank you for coming and being so prompt. So many people these days seem to think that punctuality has gone out of fashion and indeed it has, for them."

Hazel gave her 'certified as a professional' smile.

"Miss Mowbray, delighted to meet you. May I introduce my associate, Belinda Lawrence?"

Miss Mowbray transferred her gaze to Belinda, her eyes flicking over her from top to toe and back again. "How do you do?"

"Hello, Miss Mowbray, you have a magnificent home here."

Miss Mowbray twitched slightly at the mention of 'home'. Again she ran her eye over Belinda, as though she suspected her of some deliberate indiscretion.

"Home? Surely you mean, house?"

Belinda, a little startled by the woman's reaction and feeling that she was once again a school girl facing her headmistress after committing a particularly serious misdemeanour, replied: "Yes, of course, house. How stupid of me."

Miss Mowbray although clearly not satisfied with Belinda's response, transferred her interest back to Hazel.

"I believe your qualifications are in order Mrs Whitby, so if you'll come with me I will show and tell you what I require to be done." She turned and led them towards the landing where a heavy oak door, with linen fold relief carving, overlooked the space.

As they walked Belinda observed her. Miss Mowbray appeared to be in her mid-sixties, but was by no means an old lady. Slim, tall and erect, she walked quickly and with purpose, her manner abrupt and frosty. Her grey hair was cut short almost in the manner of a man's, which added to the masculine impression that Miss Mowbray presented. She wore no make-up and her face although lined was firm, while her dark eyes conveyed little of her true feelings. Dressed in a plain black dress and carrying an extraordinary number of keys of all sizes on a large key ring, she reminded Belinda of a modern Mrs Danvers.

Opening the door, Miss Mowbray led them into the Great Hall. Again, Belinda's breath was taken away at the sight. The immense hammerbeam roof arched over the room, which ran the length of the building.

At one end a large oriel window, almost floor to ceiling, looked out over the surrounding countryside, the diamond leaded glass panels illuminating the interior space with an almost otherworldly light while a burst of colour here and there came from the addition to the panels of family Coats of Arms.

A huge stone fireplace dominated the room while in the centre a highly wrought dinning table stretched almost half the length of the room. Above the fireplace hung a massive tapestry depicting an allegorical scene of the riches of the earth. Various 18th century prints, including some by Hogarth from his moral works, landscape paintings and portraits, mostly of previous family members through the ages, filled the panelled walls whereas large rugs ornately covered the wooden floor. Also on the walls were more weapons similar to those in the entrance hall: Twenty antique rifles arranged in a giant fan pattern; elaborate swords from another age their blades crossed as though frozen in battle; several large pikes, over six feet in length, their wooden shafts strengthened in part by metal strips and topped by evil looking iron spearheads.

Again, as in the solar, items of great value cluttered up the ancient space including Tudor furniture and a display of pewter dishware.

An Aladdin's cave indeed thought Belinda.

"As I indicated in our communications, Professor de Gray passed away six months or so ago. Probate has been issued and the house has been left to Heritage. Due to its great age and the fact that it has remained in the one family for so long they welcomed it, so it will be their responsibility from now on." Miss Mowbray stopped for a moment, her voice failing. With a visible effort she drew herself up and continued: "As I said the house is taken care of. It remains now to do a valuation of the contents. As you can see, there is much to consider, the furnishing and personal items reach back over four hundred years. Professor de Gray of course collected many items during his life time as well, so it will take some considerable time to complete the valuation. Do you agree?"

Hazel cast an eye around the Great Hall.

"I agree. Frankly I didn't fully realise the enormity of the task.'

Miss Mowbray turned an intimidating face to her.

"Is it beyond you? Because if it is, I would rather ..."

"No, not at all," said Hazel quickly, "it's only that it will take longer than I anticipated, but I would relish the opportunity to ..."

Before she could continue, Miss Mowbray turned and began to walk back toward the staircase.

"Good. That is settled then. Take as long as you like, but be accurate. I dislike imperfection."

Hazel decided she disliked this woman intensely but she and Belinda scuttled after her, after all she was to pay them well for their work.

As they descended the staircase, Miss Mowbray continued: "The rest of the rooms in the house are mainly bedrooms. Most of those furnishings have been removed over time but there may be some that still have items of significance. I doubt if the drapes contained in those rooms are of value and should probably be excluded as they are worn and dilapidated.

"Apart from them, there are my quarters, which are private and personal and of no interest to you. However there're also the kitchens and some storage rooms. The kitchens do have some cooking utensils of great age, which should create some interest and fetch a goodly sum. You will include them. The out houses are of no real concern to you as most of the old farm machinery is decrepit and will be removed as rubbish. The stables also have little of value. I will take you down now, to the only other room of real interest to you, which is the parlour and was used by Professor de Gray as his study."

The parlour was off the entrance hall and lay directly below the Great Hall; the huge heavy oak rafters that weighed down the low ceiling supported the enormous weight above. Old leather bound books crammed almost every available wall space and most of the floor space, and, adding to the already claustrophobic atmosphere of the room, more old weapons cluttering up every available space, including a quantity of spear heads, clubs with nails imbedded in them, some 17th century powder horns and a dangerous looking scimitar. Modern filing cabinets, a telephone, a computer, the only nod to contemporary times, were transparently out of place in this room frozen in time. An oak desk laden with documents, although neat, managed to give a confused appearance. Facing the desk was a window, more modern that others in the house, with a central glass door leading out into the garden.

"This is where the Professor did all his work. As you can see, it hasn't really been touched since his death."

"What exactly was his work?" said Hazel.

"He wrote many books on medieval history, especially religious history, and he also published works in professional journals on medical diseases, in particular mental illness during the Middle Ages. He'd been writing a new book on the death of St Thomas Becket and was very excited about it."

Belinda nodded. "There's always been interest in his murder."

Miss Mowbray flashed a questioning look at Belinda.

"You have an interest in the subject?"

"Well, not really, other than a mild curiosity about the events." Belinda felt uncomfortable again beneath the woman's gaze as though she was under suspicion of having some ulterior motive.

Apparently satisfied with Belinda's answer, Miss Mowbray continued: "Sadly he was unable to complete the book. All of his notes are in his files here and the manuscript remains on the computer. He was working on the final chapter when he passed away."

"Will it be published?" asked Hazel.

"That's still to be decided," Miss Mowbray said, busying herself with various papers on the desk. "Some publishers are interested, but it remains to be seen if we can find someone to complete the final chapter. I understand most of the research is contained in the Professor's notes, so it may be possible." She placed a document file under her arm and faced the two women. "Now, you are free to use this parlour as your work place and may come and go as you wish." She placed a set of keys on the desk. "I'm leaving straight away for London and will be gone for a short time, so I will send Mrs Day in and you can make any arrangements you wish with her. Mrs Jones, the cook, comes in to prepare lunch each day and you may let her know what you want in the way of refreshments. Only on weekdays of course, she doesn't come at weekends. Do you have any questions before I depart?"

Hazel gave a shake of her head.

"No. Everything is clear. I'm sure we will enjoy our work and I'm also sure you'll be more than satisfied with the result."

Miss Mowbray looked doubtful but gave a resolved nod.

"Very well. I will go." She turned, walked to the door, paused and turned back. "Oh, one thing. I don't have a mobile telephone – hate the things – so you won't be able to contact me until I return. If you have any urgent enquiries I suggest you contact my solicitor, Mr Fosdyke. You'll find his card with contact details somewhere on the desk." With that and a rattle of her keys, she was gone.

Belinda and Hazel looked at each other and both gave a laugh.

"One more key on that ring and she'd qualify as Mrs Danvers," said Hazel chuckling away.

"Snap! That's exactly what I thought," said Belinda. She walked over to the window and looked out at the grounds. The few rather worn-out apple trees stretching down the side of the house provided a dismal outlook.

Mrs Day bustled into the room.

"Miss Mowbray tells me you both are goin' to be here for some time and I'm to look after you. What exactly is it you're doin'?"

Hazel, decreeing that the woman was a necessary evil, gestured around the room.

"We're doing an inventory of all the furnishings and fittings in the house."

Mrs Day looked at Hazel with a jaundiced eye.

"I see. Well, rather you than me. At least I won't have to be dusting and polishing much longer."

"How long have you worked here, Mrs Day," said Belinda.

"Oh, must be thirty or so odd years. The old place was much busier then, lots of University types you know, academics and the like, full of big words and self importance. Dinner parties, cocktails in the orchard in summer. All 'go' it was. Not like recent times. The visitors now seem to be simply interested in the book the old Prof was writing."

Belinda glanced out at the bedraggled orchard.

"Not much remains of the orchard now, Mrs Day."

The woman walked over to the glass door and inspected the emaciated trees.

"Sad sight, isn't it? Of course it used to be much bigger. In fact the Manor House owned all the land around here in the real old days, a couple of hundred years or more ago I mean, but over time it's been sold off, a bit here, a bit there. Now all it has is what you see."

"Why did the dinners and parties stop?" asked Hazel. She rather liked the idea of cocktail parties in the orchard, moonlight, apple blossom and a handful of handsome young men to choose from.

"Age. Age caught up with most of the Prof's cronies and with him as well, after all he was over eighty-five but sprightly with it. Course it really fell apart when the Missus died."

"The Prof's, I mean Professor's wife?" Belinda said.

"Yes. Took a tumble down the stairs one night. Terrible fuss. She and the Prof were in the Great Hall. Having words, so it seems. She stormed out, tripped and fell. Broke her neck. The Prof was beside himself. Locked himself in his room and wouldn't come out for days. Eventually he had to, to go to the funeral. Some say he never got over it, but to my mind he seemed normal enough and was soon back into his usual routine. Mind you, a lot of his old friends didn't

13

call around after that."

Hazel fidgeted. A cigarette wouldn't go amiss about now.

"Why was that, do you think?"

Mrs Day shrugged.

"Search me. Like I said, age maybe. But there were whispers."

"About what?" said Belinda.

"Can't remember exactly, but they had something to do with the Manor House and him still living here."

"But if the house had been in the Professor's family for four hundred years …"

Before Belinda could finish, Mrs Day said, "Oh no. It wasn't the Prof's family. Oh no, it was his wife's family, the de Goderigge's. She inherited it before they married."

"And he inherited when she died," said Hazel, in a guarded voice.

"That's right," said Mrs Day, "his wife was the last of her family and the Prof and she didn't have any children."

Hazel and Belinda exchanged a glance as Hazel moved the chair out from the desk and sat down heavily. Before she could ask another question, Mrs Day said: "That's where he died."

Hazel shifted uncomfortably in the chair.

"You mean here? In this chair?"

Mrs Day nodded.

"Yes. Slumped over his desk, just there. So I was told." She pointed at the desk.

"Who found him?" said Belinda.

"Miss Mowbray. He always locked himself in here of a morning, to work on his book. At one o'clock I served him his lunch in the solar as usual. Mrs Jones prepared it and I always left the tray for him on the table there, a salad usually. Liked his salads, did the Prof. Then I came along here, knocked on the door to let him know it was lunchtime and then went about my business."

"Did he answer you?"

Mrs Day shook her head.

"Not then. Not ever. It was routine, I'd knock so he'd know it was one o'clock and that was that. He never replied. I went to collect the empty lunch dishes at two o'clock as I always did, but they hadn't been touched. Well, I thought he hadn't heard me knock, so I went and knocked again but there was no answer. I called out to him, but still no answer. I went and found Miss Mowbray and told her. She had the key to this room and she opened the door and found him, as I said, slumped over the desk."

Hazel leaned forward.

"What happened then?"

"So, Miss Mowbray came out, locked the door and went and rang Doctor Friend. He came, examined the Prof, said he was dead, probably from a heart attack – apparently he'd been seeing the doc about his ticker and the doc said it was no surprise – and then a little later, Taylor the undertaker came and took the body away."

"Did you see the body?"

"Not really. I wasn't allowed in here. But I saw them carrying him out. That's when I saw the blood on his head."

Chapter Two

Belinda ran her fingers through her dark hair as she relaxed back into the sofa in their hotel lounge.

"True, she said there was blood on his head but it's possible he hit his head when he fell. It's a pity that we weren't able to talk to Mrs Day longer than we did."

"We were there to work," said Hazel stirring her gin with a swizzle stick, "and there's always tomorrow and the next day and the next. I suspect we will be still here well into the New Year. But if you think about it, Mrs Day said he was found slumped at the desk. That wouldn't be enough to cause a head wound."

Belinda considered this.

"Yes, and we only have Miss Mowbray's word that he was slumped over the desk, apparently she kept the door closed and didn't allow Mrs Day in," said Belinda, as she picked up the dinner menu and browsed through the enticing dishes. The pumpkin soup and rack of lamb seemed ideal for a cold winter's night after their first day at work.

Hazel was thoughtful.

"Yes – I wonder why she kept Mrs Day outside in the hall, wouldn't let her into the study, after all, she was a trusted employee and you'd think that the woman would have appreciated having some support at a time like that. I mean, her employer and presumably old friend popping off suddenly, it must have been a shock, unless …"

"Unless she'd been expecting it, or …"

"Or she'd planned it," concluded Hazel, draining her glass and giving a contented sigh.

"You mean she bopped him on the head? Possibly, but why? And what exactly was Miss Mowbray's relationship with the Professor?"

"When she first contacted me she told me she was his 'secretary' and that term could cover a multitude of activities," said Hazel with a grin.

Belinda smiled. "Lovers? But he was well over eighty and she's no spring chicken."

"Old birds can be tender, provided you let them simmer for a while."

Belinda laughed. "And this is your personal philosophy?"

Hazel gave her the fish eye. She knew Belinda was teasing her but references to her age were a touchy subject.

"So, you think he let her simmer too long and didn't fancy the dish when it was served up, so she lost her temper and did him in?" continued Belinda.

"All things are possible," said Hazel somewhat tartly, "but it would be interesting to find out more about Miss Mowbray and just what her background is."

"As well as just how friendly she was with the Professor," said Belinda.

With that the two women descended upon the dining room and for the next hour or so their only thoughts were culinary but by an unspoken agreement they avoided the poultry dishes.

Miss Mowbray stepped off the tube at Embankment, into the human mass that engulfed and carried her up with it, up into the frosty London morning air. Portly older office workers eager for retirement and suburban nirvana mixed with youthful executives, spiky haired, impossibly adolescent and deluded enough into thinking they could change the world. Girls skimpily dressed in clothing more suited to a night club than the office, chattering and jabbering shrilly, pushed roughly past the older woman establishing that it was their world and she had no part in it. And indeed Miss Mowbray felt she hadn't.

At the tube station entrance Villiers Street was crowded with more of the human ebb and flow. After so many years away from London the confusion of the metropolis startled her and undermined her rigid strength of will. Miss Mowbray glanced at her watch. She was early for her appointment. She wandered into the Victoria Embankment Gardens seeking momentary relief from the hustle and bustle until she felt calmer and able to continue on her way. She slowed and meandered around the flower bed to fill in time, to have time to think. Her gloved hands held a document file. Now that she was in London she began to feel uncertain. *Should she continue on to her appointment?* It would be so easy just to descend into the earth, take the tube back to her hotel at Victoria and forget the whole thing.

A young man rushing towards the station brushed past her and knocked the file from her hand. Momentarily stunned by the collision Miss Mowbray almost gave into her temptation. She bent down and picked up the file, brushing away the dirt from the garden bed. *I'm being stupid. I haven't come this far for nothing.* Moving on, she found herself back at the garden gate, Villiers Street and a choice. Return or stay? No. It was her right, her legacy. With a firm step and head erect she turned her back on the tube station and headed off towards The Strand.

Crossing the road she passed Oscar Wilde's memorial, the writer forever waiting to engage in conversation, and into St Martin's Lane. The Duke of York's Theatre announced that their Christmas attraction was a stage version of Agatha Christie's, 'Sparkling Cyanide'. Miss Mowbray, distracted by her pressing thoughts, failed to acknowledge that the producer's choice of a murder most foul was exceptionally ill chosen for the Christmas season of good will to all men. Pressing on she came to a bland modern, red brick office building. She paused at the list of brass name plates near the entrance. Oliver & Oliver, Inc. Publishers.

Now that she had arrived at the appointed place the last shreds of indecision that had plagued her all morning faded, and steeling herself, Miss Mowbray mounted the steps and entered through the imposing glass doors.

Since she was now working in the Manor House, Hazel abandoned her haute couture mode of dress and favoured more sensible and comfortable attire consisting of warm slacks and a heavy knit pullover. These garments proved to be indispensable, as the 17th century building was decidedly arctic, without roaring fires burning in the giant fireplaces and numerous lackeys to constantly keep an eye on them and feed them hearty servings of English Oak. She had settled into the Great Hall with her laptop computer and begun in earnest to catalogue and value each and every item starting with some paintings.

A late 19th century, French romantic school oil on canvas, of country maidens by an antique water feature. £450-550.

Hazel gave a violent sneeze, shivered and wiped her nose.

A 19th century oil on panel portrait of a gentleman smoking a pipe. £150-200.

A pen & ink drawing of a young woman lying on a bed reading a book, signed, André Dunoyer de Segonzac. £500-800.

An ominous prickle began to irritate Hazel's throat.

Oil on canvas still life, study of flowers in a basket. £450-550.

Hazel gave a raspy cough and her head hurt.

And so the morning wore on.

Belinda had been assigned the task of exploring the rooms that they had so far not viewed. This proved to be an easy task as most were empty and those that were furnished contained only bedroom items of little value. Only one of these rooms had a bed that was of any significance, that being a mahogany single four-poster. The heavy gold fabric and tie backs were damaged, dusty and faded.

Late Regency, thought Belinda, dating from around 1818 or so, was her estimation.

Two large rooms appeared to have been converted into bathrooms during the Victorian period only to suffer haphazard renovations over the years, which did nothing to improve their appearance or comfort for the bather.

The rooms that had been identified as the bedrooms of the Professor and his wife also revealed little of value. There was an adjoining door between the two rooms that appeared to have been a recent innovation and was no doubt created when the Professor had married. The rooms had been stripped bare of any personal belongings and each contained nothing more than a bed and wardrobe that were reproductions of little worth and clearly manufactured in recent times. Belinda wondered what the history of the previous de Goderigge family was before the Professor's wife inherited it. Had they sold off most of the valuable original bedroom furniture? That would account for the reproduction beds.

The wardrobe doors hung open revealing wire coat hangers hung in disarray. There was a heavy air of sadness about the barren rooms and Belinda was more than satisfied to shut the door behind her and leave them to their bareness and the departed spirits of the Professor and his wife.

A storage room also proved to be disappointing, presenting clutter of relatively modern chairs, broken and in disrepair, some picture frames, a large chest almost buried under decaying fabrics, old carpets and some meagre watercolour paintings of the type displayed at amateur art exhibitions and probably dating from the early twentieth century.

Leaving these unsatisfactory rooms, Belinda came to the last one at the end of the passageway. As soon as she entered Belinda realised that she had stumbled upon Miss Mowbray's quarters. The room was provided with a hotchpotch of furniture obviously taken at random from other rooms in the house as required, including a Victorian iron frame single bed, and a large redwood wardrobe. There was the soft fragrance of lavender and roses in the air, a surprisingly feminine room for one as masculine in appearance as Miss Mowbray. A small bathroom, obviously a modern installation, was visible through an open door. On the dresser were a few personal items, a silver comb and hair brush, a perfume bottle and a photograph in a silver frame.

Full of curiosity, but feeling in the wrong by prying into Miss Mowbray's belongings, Belinda picked up the photograph. It showed a seated man on a stone fence and a woman standing nearby. The setting was a field with what appeared to be an old barn or stone building in the background. Judging by their dress it was taken many years ago.

"That's the two of them together."

Belinda turned guiltily to see Mrs Day standing in the doorway. Her arms were full of fresh bed linen. She bustled in and began to strip the sheets off the bed.

"I've been valuing the furniture in the rooms and didn't realize this one was in use," said Belinda, feeling she had to explain her presence.

"Don't worry, dear. It's not as though you'll find much in here. Keeps herself to herself, does Miss Mowbray."

Belinda looked at the photograph as she placed it back on the dresser.

"Do you mean this is the Professor and Miss Mowbray?"

Mrs Day ceased her work and shuffled around the bed to join Belinda.

"Yes, that's them."

Belinda could see that Miss Mowbray had been softer and more feminine in those days and not unattractive.

"Taken when they first met?"

"Lord no," said Mrs Day, as she gave the photograph a polish with a duster, "they met well before that. She was a student at the University and attended his lectures. They became friendly and she stayed on as his assistant."

"But how did his wife feel about that?"

"He was single then. He didn't marry until much later. I reckon it must have been thirty years or more ago. I know he'd been married just before I came to work here. I hear tell that Miss Mowbray left about the time he married but it seems she came back sometime later."

Belinda studied the Professor, and she saw a striking man, not tall or handsome, but even in the faded photograph she could sense his masculine attraction and understood why Miss Mowbray would have been fascinated.

"So he married late in life? What about his wife, was she younger or older?"

"A few years younger. A very quiet lady, refined in her way. Spoke softly. Religious, you know the type. Was always up at St Martin's church praying. She's buried up there in the churchyard. I believe in the hereafter as much as the next person, but some people take it to extremes." Having put in plain words her stance on religious conviction, she began to remake the bed.

Belinda sat on the arm of a worn armchair.

"Mrs Day, you mentioned that you saw blood on the Professor's head when he was taken away by the undertakers. Did you think it strange?"

"To tell the truth, I did. They had him in a body bag but it wasn't zipped up all the way. Gave me quite a turn. But afterwards when I went into the study I could see that Miss Mowbray had cleaned most of the blood off the desk. But there was some she'd missed. I didn't much care for cleaning it up but I did. So it looked as though he did hit his head when he collapsed."

"And what about the funeral? Were there many people there?"

"There was no funeral. He was cremated the next day."

"The next day?" said Belinda, taken aback at this news. "Why did it happen so quickly?"

Mrs Day shrugged her shoulders.

"Don't ask me. It seems the Doc issued a death certificate and arranged with the undertaker for him to be cremated next day. As far as I know, only Miss Mowbray attended at the funeral parlour." She plumped up the pillows on the bed and gathered up the used sheets. "There, that's ready for when she comes home." So saying, Mrs Day ambled out into the hall. Belinda joined her.

"Now that you mention it, it does seem odd that the funeral was rushed," Mrs Day said, as they walked back towards the parlour. "I hadn't given it much thought to be honest. I mean, he'd had a lot of friends so you think they would have wanted to pay their respects, and even the day he died there'd been people calling to see him."

Belinda looked at the woman.

"He had visitors?"

"One or two."

"Do you know who they were?" asked Belinda, her interest totally aroused.

"Well, it was six months ago. I'm not sure." They arrived at the door to the parlour. "I do know that I looked out the window from up in the solar and saw young Tommy Bedford coming through the orchard."

"Didn't he knock at the front door?"

Mrs Day gestured to the glass door set in the window.

"Didn't need to. The Prof had that door put in so his visitors could come and go without interrupting the household."

Belinda walked to the door.

"So anyone could have come in at any time and especially on that day."

"Well, one for sure was Tommy and then later on I think I saw Peter leaving, but I'm not sure. But I did hear several voices throughout the morning as I went about my business, so I guess there were other visitors. What with the Prof just about to finish his book on St Thomas, I suppose there would have been a number of interested people calling on him so I didn't really pay that much attention. I was too busy looking for Mrs Jones. She'd forgotten to put the mayonnaise on the Prof's salad but I couldn't find her, so I had to go down to the kitchen and get it myself."

"These people you saw, who …?"

"Tom Bedford," said Mrs Day with a smile, "cheeky young beggar. He's a student at the University and used to help the Prof with his research. And the other was Peter. Peter Jones, his mother works in the kitchen here. Makes your lunch for you each day." Mrs Day looked thoughtful. "Strange boy. I say boy, but he's really a man. A bit odd, like."

"In what way?"

"Well, nothing serious, you understand. He's just a bit of a loner and besotted with getting a job in the Archives up at the Cathedral. You know, where they have all the historical records and stuff. He was keen on what the Prof was writing about St Thomas."

The telephone on the desk rang and Mrs Day picked up the receiver.

"Hello? Yes, that's me." She listened to the caller and turned her head to look at Belinda, her eyes full of puzzlement. "But do you know when?" She shook her head once or twice and slowly put the receiver down.

"Now there's a peculiar thing."

"What is it, Mrs Day? You look worried," said Belinda.

"That was a call from London. A message from Miss Mowbray. It's very odd. Unusual."

"What did she say?"

Mrs Day shook her head.

"It wasn't her. No, some strange woman. She said: 'Miss Mowbray will be staying in London and she will contact you when she is coming home'."

Mark Sallinger slowed as he manoeuvred his Aston Martin Vanquish onto the exit to Dover/Canterbury road. He glanced at his watch. 4.00pm. He would be with Belinda soon and just in time for tea. He'd heard of a splendid tea shop that had been recommended to him for serving home made Maids of Honour tarts, said to rival those famed confections from Richmond, the place of their origin, and having missed lunch he was prepared to yield to a sugary indulgence.

Belinda's email had given him the address of the Manor House where she and Hazel were working. Hazel it seems had gone off early to nurse a bad head cold and he was to collect Belinda and return her to the hotel. He switched on the car headlights as the winter night began to descend in earnest.

A visit to his mother that morning had delayed him a little, but since the death of his father he had been keeping an eye on her. He chuckled to himself. *The last woman on earth who needed watching over*. His parents had been married for sixty years and although he knew his mother missed his father, she had always been strong, determined, a tower of strength and now showed no signs of weakening.

Except for the few staff she retained she was alone now in the great Jacobean country house that had been her home all her married life. Stoic and facing the future full on, she was determined to challenge whatever life threw at her. His sister Patricia, married now and living in Paris, had been a great comfort to her during the time of the funeral and the following weeks but she had returned home to tend to her own family. His mother had promised to visit but he knew she probably wouldn't. Paris was not her favourite city. Rome she favoured because of the food and it allowed her to engage in a lifelong flirtation with the Church of Rome, a flirtation that her family and friends considered to be an affectation, which indeed it most certainly was and practised as a means of creating some drama in her life which, truth to tell, she sometimes felt was disappointingly bland.

Mark's intention to marry Belinda was looked upon with some unease by his mother. She had never been discourteous to Belinda when Mark had brought her home to visit on numerous occasions but indicated in subtle ways to him that she considered it a case of 'sowing wild oats' and that in time he would be sensible, see reason and eventually marry into an established English family. One that she approved of, of course.

Mark frowned. His relationship with Belinda had been rocky at times in the past and he knew that Brad, her old boyfriend from Australia still had a place in her heart. He also knew that Brad had been in contact with her again and was urging her to return home to Australia. Belinda was at two minds about this suggestion. In one way she longed to return to Melbourne to see her parents and friends, but she could do that at any time. What Brad was suggesting was something entirely different. He had proposed marriage during his last visit to London and Mark felt sure that if Belinda did return once more to her homeland, Brad would convince her to marry him and stay there. He also knew that Belinda, uncertain as she had been, had reached a point where she knew she must decide on her future and he was determined to have her as his bride.

However there was an additional problem. His father's death had changed things a great deal and if he was determined to marry Belinda there was now a problem that faced both of them and he was not sure how Belinda would react to the news. A faint drizzle clouded the windscreen and he switched on the wipers as soft light rain swept across the darkening landscape.

In the shadowy Great Hall Belinda gave a shiver and pulled her coat tighter around her chest. The old building held the chill weather within its walls and the small bar heater that had been supplied by Mrs Day was wildly ineffectual in such a vast room. Since Hazel had fled back to the hotel and bed in an attempt to stave off her head cold, Belinda had been cataloguing the various items into the laptop awaiting Hazel's valuation.

Belinda glanced at her watch. Four-thirty. What little daylight there was had disappeared gradually under the dark rain clouds and as Mark was due soon there seemed little point in continuing working. Belinda switched off the computer, the heater and gathered her things.

Mrs Day appeared at the door.

"I'm off now. Will you be all right by yourself?"

Belinda wound her woollen scarf around her neck.

"Yes, thank you. Mark, my boyfriend, will be here soon. I'm finished here for the day and I'll wait downstairs."

"Right you are. See you tomorrow."

Mrs Day encased herself in a bright yellow and black plastic mackintosh with matching bonnet and thus reinforced against the rain, clattered off down the stairs. Belinda stood for a moment and once again looked in awe at the beauty of the Great Hall. She wondered at what scenes it had experienced in its four hundred years. Lovers kissing, marriages, lovers fighting, births, deaths, all the excitement and tragedies of human existence.

Pensively, she turned and stepped out onto the landing closing the heavy door behind her. She thought she heard the faint sound of a car but walking to a misty window that looked out over the front garden she could see nothing, only Mrs Day mounted on her bicycle forging on through the rain, looking for all the world like a giant bumblebee on the lookout for its colony and seeking shelter. Belinda smiled to herself as she turned and in the dim light began to descend the stairs, cautiously feeling her way with the hand rail as a guide. A sharp wind had blown up, splattering rain against the window panes and causing the old house to creak and grumble.

Mid-way down the stairs she stopped. An alien noise in one of the rooms below startled her. Instantly she felt apprehensive and the huge empty house, in some sinister way, threatening. She'd had just seen Mrs Day leave and Mrs Jones had long gone. Just after lunch.

Had Miss Mowbray returned unexpectedly? That seemed unlikely as Mrs Day would have known and, given Miss Mowbray's character, Belinda felt sure that the first thing she would have done upon her return would be to track down either Hazel or herself to ensure that work on the valuation was happening on schedule and she was not being cheated in any way. She also doubted if Hazel, being as ill as she was, would have returned so late in the day besides which, there was no sign of her car. Who could it be?

Further sounds followed, the rattling of doors or wooden items being moved clumsily. Tentatively Belinda moved to the bottom of the stairs and into the hall.

The noises seemed to come from the parlour. Nervous now, Belinda looked around for some form of defence should it prove necessary. A two foot long mace, with a heavy wooden shaft and a head made of iron, hung on the wall along with a small collection of other medieval weapons. Stealthily Belinda reached up and with some exertion lifted it from its fitting. The mace was heavier than she imagined and it was only with great effort that she prevented it from crashing to the ground. She paused for a moment to catch her breath.

A sharp click and a ray of light spilled out from the half closed door of the parlour. Belinda summoned up her courage and strength and lifted the mace as high as she could. She leaned forward and peered around the door.

The room was lit by a desk lamp. Silhouetted against the light was the figure of a man who was searching through files on the computer screen. Desk drawers had been opened and papers scattered about the desk.

Steeling herself, Belinda pushed open the door and, with some difficulty, lifted the mace higher.

"Who are you and what are you doing?" Her voice sounded harsh in the silent house.

The man took a quick look over his shoulder and studied Belinda. His eyes settled on the raised mace, which Belinda was struggling to hold aloft. A mischievous smirk played on his lips and he turned to face her.

"Need any help with that?"

He stepped forward and effortlessly took the mace from Belinda's grasp. She rubbed her aching arm.

"I asked who you were and what you are doing in the Professor's study," she said apprehensively, as she prepared herself to flee, now that the intruder was armed with the mace and in control of the situation.

The man dropped the weapon to the floor and sitting on the edge of the desk folded his arms across his chest and eyed Belinda from head to toe.

"I might ask you the same question," he replied smiling. "Do you always carry a weapon of mass destruction with you, or is this a special occasion?"

Belinda switched on the overhead light. The weak light revealed a young man of about twenty, tall, lean, spiky black hair, wearing the mandatory jeans of youth and a shabby leather jacket. It also revealed his mischievous hazel eyes, a fashionable wispy beard and a manner which suggested a light-hearted disposition. Handsome in a puppy-like way but, like a puppy, probably given to over enthusiastic behaviour.

"You must be the chick from London doing the evaluation."

"Not London, Bath," said Belinda, as she studied him, unsure if she could trust him but curious to know the reason for his presence in the house.

"Right. But I was told it was an old bird, so it can't be you."

"My partner is an older bir… woman," said Belinda, biting back an involuntary smile at his description of Hazel.

This seemed to satisfy the man and he bounded from the desk and advanced to Belinda with an outstretched hand.

"I'm Tom. Tommy Bedford." He grasped Belinda's hand and shook it.

"So now I know your name but I still don't know what you're doing here," said Belinda, removing her hand from his strong grip with some difficulty. She felt a little more at ease as she realised that this was the Tommy Bedford Mrs Day had mentioned and he presumably was trustworthy. But then she remembered he had been with the Professor the day he died and that thought regenerated her wariness towards him.

Tom gave a cheery smile and leaned over to the computer and switched it off.

"Just checking through some of the Prof's research for his book on Thomas Becket. I'm at the Uni and helped him from time to time. I wanted to get some details that I need for some lecture notes." He turned back to Belinda and edged closer to her looking into her eyes. "Now. You know my name, but I don't know yours," he purred in a low voice.

Belinda was amused at the unsophisticated and absurd sexual intention implicit in his manner and speech. Maybe it worked with his fellow female students. But she doubted it.

"My name's Belinda and I want to know how you got into the house." She edged away from him so that the desk was ultimately between them. Tom ignored her question.

"Belinda? Nice name. So tell me Belinda, what say you and I head into High Street, have a drink in a cool little bar I know of, and get to know each other?"

"Nice thought, but my boyfriend will be here at any minute to collect me."

Tom frowned.

"Boyfriend? You surprise me. I thought you said the old bird was your partner?"

Belinda gave him a pitying glance.

"And you assumed I meant 'life partner'?" She gave a snort of derision. "Don't tell me you have that weird male fantasy of seducing lesbians? Hazel, the old bird you refer to, is my business partner. Strictly business and if you knew Hazel you'd soon realize how wrong you were. She'd dispose of you as an entrée."

Tom shrugged and gave what Belinda later came to know as his trademark cheeky smile.

"Well, you can't win 'em all. Entrée? Maybe I'd like to meet this partner of yours. Hazel, you say?"

"Let's get back to my question. How did you get in?"

Tom produced a key ring and jiggled it in the air.

"Got a key. The Prof gave it to me, so I could come and go as I pleased." He gestured at the side glass door leading to the orchard.

"Why would he do that?" said Belinda, glancing out the door. There was a small beaten up car parked in the trees presumably Tommy's.

"Like I said, I helped him with his research on Thomas Becket. Have done for a year or so. I'm studying medieval history."

"That's a pretty broad topic. Care to be more specific?"

"Well, if you're going to be picky, non-Christians in a medieval, largely Christian culture. The Prof, although sort of retired, still gave lectures now and again, and medieval history was his speciality. When I heard he was writing a book on Becket I offered to help as he was a bit slow on the computer, like most of the oldies. He agreed and I did research with him and did some proof reading of various drafts for the book."

"So you knew all about the book?"

"Most of it. But the last chapter he kept to himself. Wouldn't let me or anyone read it, let alone know what it was about." He glanced about the room as though searching for something. "And it seems to be missing."

"Can you make a guess as to what it was about?"

Tom shrugged. "Not really. But the old boy was very excited about it. Said it was going to rewrite history."

"And you say this last chapter, which was so important, is missing. Not on the computer files or a hard copy anywhere?" said Belinda.

Tom gave a sigh.

"That's right. I can only guess that he had it on a file on a USB." He smirked. "Up until I came to help him the old boy had been using floppy disks for storing his files, so I brought him into the twenty-first century and introduced him to USB flash files. And if that's the case and that's where it's stored, the USB file being so small, only and inch or so, it could be anywhere."

"And you were looking for it," said Belinda, accusingly.

Tom's smile shone forth again.

"Now why would I be doing that?"

Belinda decided to make known her suspicions about the Professor's death and see what Tommy's reaction would be.

"Because from what I've heard, what's on the file might be valuable and worth quite a lot of money. Maybe even worth killing for."

Tommy raised a questioning eyebrow and then the smile on his face twisted into a sneer.

"Killing for? Has anyone been killed?"

Belinda looked closely at the young man opposite her.

"It's a possibility that the Professor might have been murdered."

Tom gave an over hearty raucous laugh.

"You're nuts. The old boy had a bad ticker and just kicked the bucket."

Belinda felt that his response was a little too practised, too glib.

"True," said Belinda, "he might have had a bad heart, but its possible someone helped him to 'kick the bucket' as you say, with a blow on the head."

At that moment the room was filled with light as Mark arrived and the headlights of his car flooded the room. In that instant Belinda saw Tom's face devoid of any smile and replaced now with a look of extreme hostility.

Chapter Three

"Are you listening to me?" Belinda rapped the tea room table. Mark had appeared distracted since his arrival in Canterbury and seemed more interested in the Maid Of Honour tarts than in her telling of the events at the Manor House. He had eaten two of the confections and was reaching for his third. "You seem to be more concerned with your stomach than in what I've been telling you."

Mark wiped the flakes of pastry from his chin and took a mouthful of tea.

"I'm hungry, that's all. So this landlady has gone missing?"

Belinda gave a shrug of annoyance. Really, Mark could be so exasperating went he wanted.

"Not a landlady. Miss Mowbray was the Professor's secretary. She went up to London on some business and hasn't returned. Just sent a message that she would be away for a while."

"So?" said Mark, contemplating the remaining tart. Belinda saw this look and moved the plate out of his reach.

"So," said Belinda irritably, "why did she suddenly decide to stay in London?"

"Maybe she just wanted to have a holiday. See the sights. Take in a show. People do, you know."

Belinda gave a petulant shake of her head. She hated to admit it but Mark was right. Maybe there was no mystery. They rose and Mark paid the bill. A chill breeze assaulted them as they stepped out into Sun Street and headed back to the hotel.

"Well, you may be right about Miss Mowbray, except Mrs Day thought it was strange behaviour and then there's the murder."

"What murder?" said Mark, pulling a woollen scarf tight around his throat to ward off the sudden gust of bitter wind. Belinda gave a groan of irritation. Mark wasn't taking any of this seriously.

"I told you when you arrived. The Professor was hit on the head."

"You mean, you think he was hit on the head, but you have no proof."

"Mrs Day saw the blood on his head," said Belinda defensively.

Mark gave her a sidelong glance.

"And that proves he was murdered?"

Belinda pursed her lips in annoyance. But she had to admit that Mark was right. Again. Perhaps she had been overzealous in assuming that a crime had been committed.

They arrived at the hotel, checked on Hazel but were met with a 'Do Not Disturb' sign on the door handle, which by some means conveyed to the reader in those few words Hazel's prickly personality and guaranteed misery to anyone who was foolish enough to step over the threshold. She had obviously decided to take to her bed until the annoying head cold had been cured. Belinda and Mark retreated to the lounge and sank down on the comfortable sofa.

"I think it would be best if you started at the beginning and told me everything that has happened," said Mark. And so Belinda began at the beginning and regaled Mark with what had happened in the past few days and most of what she had discovered about the Professor, Miss Mowbray and the missing chapter from the book on St Thomas Becket.

The Lancashire Hot Pot and pickled red cabbage had assuaged Mark's hunger so, as they lingered over coffee and port, he felt free to evaluate Belinda's observations.

"The key to it all is to find the missing USB file. That way we can see what all the fuss is about," he said as he sipped his coffee.

"So you believe me now when I say there's a mystery surrounding the Manor House and the Professor's death?" said Belinda complacently, feeling somewhat satisfied that she had been correct all along.

Mark reached over, took her hand, kissed it and gazed into her eyes.

"Darling, I never doubted you for a moment."

Despite the mocking look in Mark's eyes and his mischievous smile, Belinda smiled back. *He really is so handsome. I'm a fool not to marry him.* Coming back to the matter in hand Belinda said: "So what do we do?"

"Let's look at what we know," said Mark. "Firstly, the Professor is writing a book, the final chapter of which, he says, contains explosive facts. The file containing that chapter has gone missing. The question is: if it is so important who, if they knew of its existence, would be prepared to kill the Professor. And why?"

"To prevent its publication?" said Belinda.

"Or to profit from its publication. Both could be considered valid reasons to bump off the Prof. And does the murderer have the file? Just what could be so electrifying in that chapter to have caused all this carry-on? After all, there've been hundreds of books published on Thomas Becket and what there is to know, is known. We can only speculate on the supposed revelations, so let's look at who the suspects are."

"Well, there's Miss Mowbray," said Belinda, doubtfully.

"Motive?" asked Mark.

"None that I can think of. It seems likely she'd been his lover years ago and had stayed with him as a friend and as his secretary. I imagine she still held a torch for him. Hardly a reason to kill him."

"What about the household staff?"

Belinda gave a smile.

"Housekeeper, Mrs Day. Pretty much down to earth. Not the sort to go around murdering people. Besides, I can't think of any reason that she'd have to get rid of the Prof. She'd likely loose her job when and if he died and I doubt if she'd have any interest in the book he was writing. Romance novels at best would probably be to her taste. As for Mrs Jones in the kitchen. Well, physically not up to it I'd say. She's like a thin timid bird and again I can't see that she'd have a motive."

Mark frowned. "Right. Who else is there? What about that student. Tim?"

"No. Tom, not Tim. Tom Bedford. According to him he'd helped the Professor with research for the book. When I found him in the parlour today he said he was searching on the computer for some information in the Prof's notes. But he seemed to know that the final chapter was on the missing USB file."

"And you told me he had a key to the parlour, which means that he could come and go at any time."

"That's right. Plus we only have his word that he was searching for information. But if so, what information and was it truly related to his Uni studies or a clue to where the missing file is hidden? If he had been working closely with the Prof, he may have some idea of what the final chapter contains, although he denies it."

Mark took a sip of port.

"Who else was there at the house on the day the Professor died?"

"Mrs Day said she saw Tom and also she thought Peter Jones was there. His mother is the cook, Mrs Jones, and he's keen on working at the Archives here at the Cathedral."

"Right, so we have two possible suspects. Tommy and Peter. What other suspects could there be?"

"Possibly some other visitors Mrs Day didn't see. They could have come in through the orchard door and she wouldn't have known."

"According to what you told me, Miss Mowbray said there were plans for the book to be published and assuming that to be true there would be a publisher."

"She said 'some publishers'. It could be two or more," said Belinda. "And Mrs Day did say she heard several voices."

Mark gave a nod.

"True. One could have been trying to outbid the others, which means that all of them would have some idea of what the missing chapter revealed and assumed it would be a historical sensation and worth a lot of money to them."

"There're also the doctor and the undertaker," said Belinda. "Let's not forget them."

"How do they fit in?" Mark said.

"Well, according to Mrs Day, the doctor wrote out the death certificate almost on the spot and the Professor was cremated the next day. Just a trifle hasty, don't you think?"

"Unusual, yes. So it's possible that the doctor and the undertaker were there earlier on in the day, before the Prof died and Mrs Day heard their voices? Perhaps we should have a talk with them."

"And maybe we shouldn't rule out Miss Mowbray. Hazel thinks she's guilty, but then Hazel thinks everyone is guilty of something."

"Right," said Mark, "that gives us five potential suspects, plus the possibility of an unknown number of publishers. What about the Cathedral Archives, did anyone there know about the book?"

"It's possible, but they haven't been mentioned, although as I told you, Peter Jones is keen to work there and he may have mentioned it in passing." Belinda laid her napkin on the table as they rose to leave the restaurant. "And there's Miss Mowbray's disappearance. I know you think she's just having a holiday, but Mrs Day thought it was out of character for her, she'd only been away once or twice before and each time that was only for a day, and she didn't leave the phone message. It was a strange woman. Why didn't she make the call herself?"

Hazel drifted in and out of consciousness. She had been dreaming and as she finally forced her eyes open some irritating fragments of the illusion swirled around in her brain. The heating in the room had been turned up and she had piled on extra blankets in an effort to reduce her cold that had settled on her chest. In a lather of perspiration she threw back the covers and reached out for a nearby glass to quench her thirst. The glass contained brandy, not her favourite tipple, but in the case of a cold or flu she felt brandy was the ideal tonic. She downed the contents and grimaced as the liquor burned her sore throat. She lay back on the pillows, exhausted. What was it she had been dreaming about? Flashes of the dream returned only to exasperatingly vanish: the Great Hall, antique furnishings, Mrs Day. Mrs Day? Yes, the housekeeper and with that Hazel recalled what had been tormenting her.

Earlier that day as she sat sneezing and coughing in the freezing Great Hall, little by little increasing her systematic valuation of the possessions contained in the Manor House, Mrs Day had bustled in and while dusting and polishing she had been chatting away like an energetic parrot. Hazel hadn't really been listening as she had made her mind up to quit work for the day and tend to her cold. But Mrs Day had said something that finally made Hazel prick up her ears.

"That's what really upset her, of course. Not getting the house."

"Who are you talking about?" asked Hazel, closing her laptop and turning off the useless bar heater.

"Why, Muriel Mowbray of course." Mrs Day turned to look at Hazel, who gave a raucous cough. "You should take care of that cold, dear. This weather has been known to carry elderly people off."

Hazel glared at the woman.

"I don't consider myself elderly, if you don't mind." She sniffed and blew her nose.

"No, dear. That's right," muttered Mrs Day, sceptically.

"So what was it you were saying about Miss Mowbray?"

Mrs Day began to polish a chair vigorously.

"Well, her being such a great friend of the Professor for such a long time and given that she had once been, well, you know, his lady friend so to speak, she naturally assumed that he had left her the house in his will. In fact he had told her so it seems, or at least that's what she said."

"Did he tell her this before or after his wife died?"

Mrs Day stopped polishing and gave Hazel a look.

"What are you suggesting?"

Hazel sniffed. "I'm not suggesting anything." But privately she thought it would make a big difference if the suggestion was made before the death of the Professor's wife.

Mrs Day gave an unconvinced grunt and resumed polishing.

"Anyway, she found a new will had been made that gave the house to Heritage and only left her the contents."

Hazel glanced around the room.

"You mean all this?"

Mrs Day glanced at her.

"That's right, and she was none too pleased I can tell you and, what's more, made sure the Professor knew it. Everything you see in the house belongs to her." She stood erect, shook out the polishing cloth and said meaningfully, "That's why she's got you doing the valuation. In my opinion she wants to know just how much she can sell it for."

"I told him his heart could give out at any time, but he just laughed and said he was made of sterner stuff," said Doctor Friend.

Late the next morning, accompanied by church bells summoning the faithful to worship, Belinda and Mark had made their way in the weak winter sunlight through West Gate and along St Dunstan's Street to London Road. Opposite St Dunstan's church was a Georgian house with a notice indicating that surgery hours were from 2.00pm to 5.00pm Monday to Friday.

A rather surly teenage girl had answered their knock at the door and informed them that the Doctor didn't see patients on a Sunday, as the notice clearly stated, and hadn't they seen it? Eventually she absorbed the information that it was no medical emergency but a personal visit and after vanishing for five minutes returned and led them to a small greenhouse attached to the rear of the house. It was there that Belinda and Mark discovered Dr Murray Friend repotting an orchid. He was a robust man in his mid-forties, thinning grey hair and displaying a self-satisfied manner.

"And of course his heart did just give up. All very well thinking you're tough but when the old ticker decides it's time to go, then it's time to go." The Doctor paused in his labours and looked back at his visitors. "Were you related in any way? I thought the old boy had no family."

"No," said Belinda, and explained that she and Hazel had been employed by Miss Mowbray to assess and catalogue all the contents of the house. Dr Friend paused from cutting decaying roots away from a plant and looked thoughtful.

"Yes. Miss Mowbray. She was a little disappointed."

"Disappointed?" said Mark, "How was she disappointed?"

But the Doctor went on as though he hadn't heard: "So then, if you're not family why this interest in the Professor's death?"

"Curiosity," said Belinda.

The Doctor tipped some broken clay pot-pieces into an empty pot, shook them and looked at Belinda uneasily.

"Curiosity killed the cat."

"We were told that he had a head wound," continued Belinda.

The Doctor abandoned his orchids and faced them, his face beginning to flush in annoyance.

"Firstly, I don't see what any of this has to do with you and secondly I don't see why I should be expected to give you any answers. I'd been his doctor for over ten years. I knew his condition and was treating him for it. He was far too energetic for a man of his age, particularly with a heart problem. He was always rushing off to some mausoleum somewhere in Bedfordshire, of all places, and fossicking about in old ruins. Much too energetic. As for the wound on his head, that was caused when he collapsed. Hit the desk when he fell. It's all in the death certificate, though I don't know why I should be bothered with telling you."

"Bedfordshire? Why did he rush off there?

"Some family connection, I gather. But all a waste of time in my opinion. Now, if you don't mind, I want to get on with my repotting." Scowling, he turned back to the plants.

"One more thing," said Mark, "he was cremated the next day. Wasn't that rather sudden?"

The Doctor dumped an orchid rather unceremoniously into a pot.

"That was what he wanted," snapped the Doctor through tight lips. "Taylor knew it as well." He gestured in the direction of the building next door. "The old boy had paid for his funeral in advance, with certain instructions. If you doubt me, ask Taylor. His parlour's just there."

"Useful," said Mark sardonically, "for patients I mean, having an undertaker next door to a doctor."

Dr Friend, now on the verge of an apoplexy glared at Mark.

"Get out!" he shouted, "Get out, the two of you before I call the police."

He rushed them to the front of the house and slammed the door after them. From a window he watched them as they crossed the road towards St Dunstan's Church. Certain that they had gone he reached for the telephone and while attempting to get his anger under control pressed a number, waited uneasily until he had an answer, and said: "There might be a problem."

Belinda and Mark stood in the grounds of the church near the Celtic Cross War Memorial and looked back at the Doctor's surgery and the gloomy funeral parlour next door. As they watched, the parlour door opened and a tall, reedy figure dressed entirely in black hurried across the road and made its way through the ancient graveyard. It was a man whose age Belinda felt hard to gauge but his dress was almost from another era, a long black frock coat, a heavy woollen scarf and a battered top hat. He reminded Belinda of one of Dickens's characters sketched by George Cruikshank. They watched him weave his way through the tombstones until he vanished behind the church.

"Do you think that's Taylor, the Funeral Director?" Belinda laughed. "Everyone wants to be a director."

"More likely someone who worked for Burke and Hare," said Mark smiling, "and maybe he's on his way to rob a grave now. But I think we will have to visit Mr Taylor at some time. I don't buy that story that the Professor requested he be disposed of so quickly. Plus, I'm curious to know what happened to his ashes."

Mark led her into St Dunstan's church. They stood in the side chapel before the stained glass window that showed events from the life of St Thomas More.

"More lost his head when he disagreed with Henry VIII over his marriage to Anne Boleyn," said Mark. "His head was parboiled and stuck up over London Bridge."

"You realise you're putting me off my lunch, don't you?" said Belinda with a shudder.

But Mark was enjoying his ghoulish homily.

"After a month with the birds pecking at it, his daughter, Margaret Roper, bribed the man who was about to throw it into the Thames."

"Where is it now?" said Belinda.

"Here in the family vault, but I gather the skull is now just crumbling bits of bone."

They left the church and began to stroll back towards West Gate.

"As the Professor's book was about St Thomas Becket," said Belinda, "I'd like to see the spot where Becket was murdered."

The Sung Eucharist had finished, the Archbishop had departed after farewelling his flock and groups of worshipers lingered behind in the Nave chatting, the women each privately and critically evaluating the winter fashions worn by their female acquaintances, the men hoping there would be time for a pint before Sunday lunch, that is if the women ever stopped their confounded prattle.

A smattering of tourists began to descend upon the Cathedral and among them, Belinda and Mark. They walked up the Nave to the Choir Screen and down into the North West transept, the site of Thomas's murder, the Martyrdom. Stained glass images of the Royal Family looked down on the now peaceful scene but the awareness of the tragedy was retained within the ancient walls.

Belinda gave a shiver, not from the cold, but from the sight of the torn Cross: the broken blades and two jagged swords that made up the Altar of the Sword's Point, marking the spot where Thomas fell. Reading about the event in school was one thing, to actually stand on the spot was overwhelming. The ramifications of the event had been world shattering.

"Thomas and the King were close friends once, I remember," said Belinda, "but they had a falling out."

"Yes," said Mark, "Henry the Second. In a nutshell, he made Becket Archbishop of Canterbury thinking that as he was an old friend, he would have him in his pocket in his plans to take certain powers away from the Church."

"It's all coming back to me now," said Belinda. "He wanted the civil courts to have more clout over the clergy. But Thomas told him to bug off and sided with the Church."

"Elegantly put," said Mark with a smile. "The King was miffed and made it clear that Thomas was a pain in the bum. Four of his knights decided to take things into their own hands and burst in here about this time of the year, Christmas or just after, December 1170, and hacked Thomas to death. Henry came to the Cathedral later and was thoroughly thrashed as penance for his role in the affair."

As he said this he led Belinda up the stairway, worn down by the thousands and thousands of pilgrims who'd made their way over the centuries, leading to the site of Becket's shrine in the Trinity Chapel.

"The monks collected Thomas's blood and soon there were reported miracles, Thomas was declared a Saint and eventually his relics were placed in a shrine here where this candle is burning. It became popular for pilgrims seeking cures and spiritual aid, Chaucer and all that."

"What happened to the shrine?" asked Belinda, as she gazed at the forlorn candle fluttering silently on the floor of the great Cathedral.

"We can blame Henry the Eighth. He had it demolished at the Dissolution of the Monasteries. Probably because Thomas represented the power of the Church over that of the King, which didn't sit well with Bluff Hal."

They walked back to the site of the murder and looked up at the windows above.

"It's ironic," said Mark, pointing to the images of Queen Elizabeth II and family, "that the English Monarchy still looks down on the murder site in stained glass captivity."

"And Thomas's remains?"

"Ah, that's an interesting question," said Mark as they walked to the Choir. "No one really knows. Bluff Hal is supposed to have decreed that the remains be destroyed. Some say they were burned, others that the monks rescued them, but there are many theories although the consensus seems to be that they were destroyed."

Belinda looked up at the magnificent kaleidoscope of stained glass windows surrounding them, many depicting miracles attributed to St Thomas.

"So what was it that excited the Professor, and so secret that he hid the final chapter of his book?"

"It could have been anything," said Mark, "maybe he discovered that the rumours of Thomas's birth were true."

They strolled out of the Cathedral and into Burgate to pause at the window of a gift shop filled with suggested Christmas gifts as well as souvenirs of the City and the Cathedral. Belinda pushed open the door and, with Mark following, entered the lair designed to trap tourists into parting with their money.

"I'll buy something to send to my mother," said Belinda, inspecting a range of items from tea cups to glass balls that, when shaken, trapped miniature cathedrals in a constant snow storm. A tea towel bearing images of St Thomas, although bordering on sacrilege, seemed the most acceptable and easiest to post by mail. Belinda handed her selection to one of the two women behind the counter.

"You're Australian, aren't you?" said the woman jovially, as she began to wrap the towel in gift paper. Her companion joined in, equally cheerily.

"We could tell from your accent. We watch your soaps, Neighbours and Home and Away on TV, so we can tell." The two women in their mid-sixties, grey haired, ruddy cheeked and plump, beamed at them. The green and red Elf hats they wore at a jaunty angle only added to their good-humoured appearance.

The first one said: "Are you visiting?"

The second said with a big smile at Mark: "Are you on your honeymoon?"

Clearly she had a romantic nature. Belinda and Mark exchanged an amused glance.

"No. We're working here at the moment," said Belinda, smiling.

This nugget of information only sparked the women's interest further.

"Working?" they queried in unison.

Belinda, amused at their curiosity, nodded.

"Yes, we're doing a valuation on some possessions."

It was plain that the women weren't going to be satisfied with that answer. Their raised eyebrows and questioning eyes demanded satisfaction. Belinda weakened.

"At the Manor House, for a Miss Mowbray."

Two pair of judgemental eyes exchanged a knowing glance.

"Oh, Miss Mowbray," said the first woman. "Well, yes. We know about her."

"All about her," added her companion. Seemingly satisfied with this information the women appeared to lose interest and the sale of the tea towel was concluded. Bemused by their questioning and behaviour, Belinda and Mark stepped out into the street.

"What was all that about?" said Belinda.

Mark laughed. "Just a couple of old biddies eager for gossip."

The morning sunshine was waning and grey clouds began to trespass on the skyline. Belinda hugged her coat tightly around her.

"You said something before, in the Cathedral, about St Thomas's birth?"

Mark turned up his collar and put his hands deep into the warmth of his coat pockets.

"There was a story, really a myth, that his mother was a high born Syrian princess who fell in love with Thomas's father when he was in the Holy Land on a Crusade."

Belinda considered this.

"Do you think it's possible that the Professor found evidence that this was actually true?"

"All things are possible," said Mark, as he took Belinda's arm and guided her back to their hotel.

If it was true, thought Belinda, *was it a discovery important enough to kill for?*

Chapter Four

Miss Mowbray emerged from Knightsbridge tube station. It was midmorning and most of the office workers had arrived at their offices and begun their new working week so the crowds surrounding her now were impatient shoppers, grim faced and uncharitable as they bemoaned the fact that they hadn't shopped early for Christmas. Just what did you give someone who has everything? The decorative lights festooning Harrods gleamed in the misty morning, a cornucopia promising treasures beyond the dreams of avarice and luring in those desperate enough now to overindulge on their credit card. Miss Mowbray found it easy to ignore the commercial siren's song, crossed the street and proceeded along Brompton Road away from the unrelenting temptation.

Her appointment was near Gloucester Road, but she needed to clear her mind before her appointment and walking helped her do that. Besides she had fond memories of student gatherings in Brompton Square. The people she had met there. The famous. The infamous. Now, few of those names meant anything. She paused at the Square for a moment of reflection. Little had changed; it could have been only yesterday that she was last there but she knew it to be, oh, how many, many years?

The Oratory nearby loomed large and Miss Mowbray was temped to wander in. She had often attended Mass there on a Sunday all those years ago. The hymns and the incense she'd found uplifting and enchanting. She wondered about confession. Was it possible to erase sin that easily? It would be nice to think such an easy solution was available. But she sensed there were some transgressions, some terrible crimes, for which sinners needed to feel pain, extreme pain before the stain on the soul could be expurgated.

She hurried on and past the familiar ornate façade of the Victorian and Albert Museum. Walter and she had often gone there when as a student she'd clung to his every word. And to him. He'd been excited by the display of the Becket Casket made for the Relics of Becket, with its gleaming Limoges enamel and the images of the Saint's life. A lifetime ago. And now Walter was dead. *Betrayed. No other word for it.*

The mist turned into a drizzle and Miss Mowbray hastened on. She left the tumult of Cromwell Road behind as she turned into

Gloucester Road and soon found herself in the calm of Cornwall Gardens. The bland face of the endless terrace façade stretched before her but the brass plate on the gate confirmed she had arrived at her destination. 'Quentin Frazer. Trad Press Publisher'

She glanced up at the first floor. He was standing at the window watching her. She pushed open the Iron Gate and made her way to the front door.

'Thomas. A New Evaluation by Professor Walter de Gray MA PhD.' The title page appeared on the computer screen. Belinda placed two cups of coffee on the desk and sat beside Mark.

"All the chapters are there, apart from the final one, which is the one we want," Mark said as he reached for his coffee, stood up, stretched, walked to the door and looked into the orchard. The parlour was dim in the late afternoon light and he switched on the overhead light. Belinda sipped her coffee. Mark had spent the afternoon reading through the Professor's book stored on his computer.

"Was the file hard to find?"

"No. Very easy. Marked, *Final Draft Saint Thomas*. Anyone could have opened the file and read it."

"Was there anything about it that was unusual? Sensational?"

Mark shook his head.

"I skimmed through it but from what I could see it was pretty much what's already been published about Becket. Miss Mowbray was wrong when she told you that there were research notes that gave details of the secret. Whatever the Prof was on about he kept for the last chapter."

Both were silent for a moment.

"OK," said Belinda, "let's consider again those we think had an interest in the missing chapter. Firstly, what about publishers? Miss Mowbray mentioned publishers. Do we know who they are?"

Mark moved back to the computer. He clicked on 'documents' and scrolled down the list stopping at 'contacts'.

The open file revealed a disorganised list of names and address. Among them they found 'Sir Justin Oliver, Publisher' and 'Quentin Frazer, Publisher' both with address and telephone number but no other publisher was listed.

"I think we can safely assume that the Prof had selected them as the two most likely prospects and offered them the book for publication," said Mark, loading their details into his mobile phone address book. "Maybe holding out for whoever made the best offer, and playing one off against the other, particularly if he'd indicated that he had some sensational new discovery concerning Becket."

"Do you think the Prof told them what it was?"

Mark looked doubtful.

"I suspect he only told them enough to get them fired up sufficiently to want to publish. He'd give them the full details after he'd got the best deal."

"So they both could have been here the day he died?" said Belinda.

Mark nodded. "We can add them to the list along with the Doctor, the Undertaker, Peter Jones and the student, Tommy."

"Tommy," echoed Belinda, "I wonder how we can find him. Check the contacts in the computer again."

Mark scrolled down the file.

"Here it is, University of Kent. Thomas Bedford. There's a mobile telephone number. We can try that. That leaves Miss Mowbray. The more I think about it, the more I feel she's not a suspect, so I think we can dismiss her."

"I wouldn't be that hasty." A harsh voice from the door startled them and they turned to see Hazel as she entered.

"Hazel, you're feeling better?" said Belinda.

Hazel gave her a look that would sour milk and coughed violently.

"Do I look or sound better?" She scowled. "No, but I'm supposed to be doing a job and lolling about in a sick bed isn't going to get it done." She collapsed into a chair at the desk and cast a malevolent eye over her young companions. "I suppose a gin and tonic is out of the question?"

Belinda laughed. Hazel was getting better.

"Sorry, no gin. But I can get you an orange juice."

Hazel's frosty reception to this proposition indicated all too clearly that Belinda may as well not waste her time.

"What did you mean we shouldn't dismiss Miss Mowbray as a suspect?"

"Because Muriel Mowbray thought she stood to inherit the house," wheezed Hazel, "but her old boyfriend did the dirty on her and without her knowing, changed his will leaving her only the contents."

Tom Bedford placed the coffee cups on the café table and leered suggestively at Belinda.

"I knew you couldn't stay away from me." Belinda and Mark exchanged a glance. They had driven out to the University and at Tommy's suggestion met him for coffee. "Lucky you caught me, the term's finished and I'm helping out in a book shop. I'm going home for Christmas tomorrow."

"Where's home," said Belinda, as she moved her thigh out of range of Tommy's, which had rubbed enthusiastically against hers.

Tommy winked over the top of his cup.

"Sevenoaks, but I'll be back for New Year's Eve. There's a party planned and if I play my cards right, I'll score."

"No doubt," said Mark coldly, "but do you mind if we ask you a few questions about Professor de Gray?"

"Fire away," said Tommy, with his eyes fixed securely on Belinda. She shifted uncomfortably under his gaze.

"You said that you'd helped him with his book."

Tommy gave a nod but no acknowledgment to Mark.

"We've been told that he often went visiting to Bedfordshire. Did that have anything to do with his claims about St Thomas?"

Tommy reluctantly let his gaze slip from Belinda and for the first time he looked at Mark.

"Not that I know of. He'd been going there for years apparently. But I drove him up there quite a few times."

Belinda leaned forward.

"What did he do there?"

Tommy turned his attention gratefully back to her and looked into her eyes.

"Not much. Would you like to come to the New Year's party? I can guarantee you a good time."

Belinda gave a sigh of annoyance.

"Just answer the question. What did he do in Bedfordshire?"

Tommy took a sip of coffee.

"Can you make it worth my while?"

His foot rubbed against Belinda's.

Mark suddenly reached across the table and grabbed the youth by his collar.

"It'll be worth a fat lip if you don't stop ogling my fiancé, you little worm. Now, just answer her question."

He let go and Tommy fell back in his chair.

"OK, guv," he said mockingly, "don't get your knickers in a twist." He once more looked at Belinda, but this time without his usual ham-fisted attempt at seduction. "I drove him to Flitton. It's a small village in Bedfordshire. There's a mausoleum attached to the church."

"What was special about that?" asked Mark.

"It's the de Grey Mausoleum. There's generations of the de Grey family buried there. Dates back to the seventeenth century or thereabouts. The old Prof looked upon them as his ancestors."

"And were they?" said Belinda.

Tommy shook his head.

"Not likely. He had the same name but a different spelling, so if you ask me, I don't think there was any real family connection, or one that he could confirm. The last de Grey died way back when, and his heir was a daughter, who lived somewhere in Hertfordshire. I think it was just wishful thinking as far as the old boy was concerned. Fancied the idea of having a titled family. One of them was Archbishop of York back in the thirteenth century. He liked that. But he went to Flitton regularly. Had done so for years. Liked to wander about looking at the memorials."

"Was that all he did there?" said Mark.

"Mostly, but sometimes he'd have me drive him over to Bushmead Priory."

"Where's that," said Belinda.

"A few miles away. It was a small priory built in the twelfth century. Only a handful of monks ever lived there. It was sold off when Henry Eight spat the dummy and later someone screwed it up by adding a Georgian façade. They demolished that over fifty years ago, that's when the old boy helped."

"With the demolition?" said Belinda.

"Well, it was more of an archaeological dig for him. Said he found lots of items of interest. Bones and bits of medieval rubbish."

"Why did he go back?"

"Who knows? Nostalgia. Knew some of the locals from the old days. But he enjoyed the dig. He was much younger then of course but was always banging on about it."

Mark and Belinda considered this.

"Well," said Mark, "I've read through the Professor's book on his computer and there doesn't appear to be anything new there. What could he have possibly discovered? Becket's bones were destroyed."

"The bones may not have been destroyed," said Tommy.

"What do you mean?" asked Belinda, with keen interest.

"Some say they're still in the Cathedral," replied Tommy, waving his hands in the air in a mock spooky gesture.

"That's news to me," said Mark sourly.

Tommy gave an amused look to them both.

"Tell you what. Meet me at the Cathedral in the North West Transept this evening. Evensong will be on, but one of the advantages of being a history student here is that I have free access to come and go at the Cathedral."

"That little creep needs a boot up the arse," growled Mark, as he slid into the driver's seat. Belinda, next to him, buckled up her seat belt.

"Oh, don't let him upset you, at least, not on my behalf. It's all bluff with him. Juvenile games."

Mark was not convinced.

"Well, just make sure he doesn't overstep the mark and lay a hand on you."

He steered the car out of the University car park and along to Whitstable Road.

Belinda looked at his strong profile.

"You called me your fiancé," she said softly.

"Did I?" was Mark's abrupt reply. Clearly his mind was elsewhere. "Seeing we are so close, we may as well call in on Taylor, the undertaker and see what he can tell us." He glanced at his watch. "That'll fill in time before Evensong and whatever it is that the little worm's got up his sleeve."

Belinda grinned.

"Worms don't have sleeves."

But her sense of humour was lost on Mark who clearly had been annoyed by Tommy's behaviour. They drove on in silence. Belinda's mind went back over Tommy's telling of the Professor's visits to the Mausoleum. She made up her mind that they should visit it, but now wasn't a good time to suggest it. She glanced at Mark. His brow forecast stormy weather so, with a secret smile, she sank back in her seat and transferred her interest to the passing scenery.

Fiancé? She found she preferred that to 'girlfriend'.

Mr Taylor looked more like a bank manager than a funeral director, which seemed fair enough thought Belinda as funerals were considered big business these days. Going grey at the temple and impeccably dressed in a dark suit, he straightened his silk tie as though one perceived imperfection in his appearance would undermine his living customers' confidence – the dead could go hang.

It was clear that Mark's fractious mood hadn't changed and he glared at the man who smoothed his hair while regarding his visitors with an air of condescension. Belinda was reminded of two stags preparing for battle at rutting season.

"Yes. I've heard of you two." Mr Taylor communicated in those few words an impression of total enmity.

Belinda hoped he showed more diplomacy when consoling weeping widows. She created a mental picture should he reveal his true feelings. 'Heard your old man karked it, love. Sorry about that. A burial you say? That'll be £3000, up front if you don't mind. Flowers an extra £200.'

"No doubt you heard from your hearty neighbour, the good Doctor," snapped Mark cynically, warming to the battle ahead.

Mr Taylor ignored him and took his place behind his desk. The office had all the charm of the graveyard complete with artificial flowers and a selection of hideous cremation urns nonchalantly awaiting human ash.

"I won't ask you to take a seat, as you will not be staying."

"Only long enough to ask why you collaborated with the doctor to cremate Professor de Gray so soon after his death."

The undertaker chose not to look at Mark, but opened a diary on his desk and said in an unruffled voice: "Are you suggesting there was some impropriety in my action?"

"There might have been if it was done to cover up a crime." Mark's irritation grew at his opponent's unresponsive manner.

Mr Taylor cast a cold eye over Mark.

"Your suggestion is outrageous and if you don't leave I shall call the police."

He reached for the telephone. Mark beat him to it and held his hand firmly on the receiver.

"Before you do, just answer my question."

The man was silent for a moment as though gathering his thoughts.

"Dr Friend advised me that the Professor, his patient, had died suddenly of a heart attack. We removed his remains from the Manor House and the doctor issued a death certificate. I was told that the deceased had left instructions that he was to be cremated as soon after death as possible and this was confirmed by his secretary, Miss Mowbray."

"Do you have that in writing?" demanded Mark harshly.

Mr Taylor ignored his interruption and went on: "There being no legal impediments to this request, his remains were transported to the Crematorium over in Charing the next day. Now, if you wish to accuse me, or the doctor, of committing a crime, that is another matter and one that I would wish to place in the hands of the police."

The two men stared at each other defiantly.

Belinda, recognizing that Mark had handled the interview badly, took his arm and moved towards the door.

"Thank you, Mr Taylor. Just one other thing. What happened to the Professor's ashes? Were they scattered somewhere?"

Mr Taylor busied himself with some papers to indicate he was bringing the meeting to a close.

"I believe the cremated remains were placed in the possession of Miss Mowbray at her request. Now as we have nothing else to say to each other, other than for me to remind you of the laws of slander, I'll ask you both to leave and suggest that you cease making these outrageous accusations."

Mark, frustrated and angry at himself for his mishandling of the situation, shook off Belinda's hand and stormed out of the office. Belinda followed with one final glance back at the undertaker.

As soon as he heard the front door close he reached for the telephone and punched in a number.

Outside, Mark stormed to his car leaving Belinda to scurry after him and she just had time to clamber in before he took off at a furious rate.

"Slow down, idiot," she cried, as they roared into St Dunstan's Street and headed towards West Gate. She glared at Mark. Feeling her angry gaze he slowed to the speed limit but gripped the driving wheel firmly, a determined jaw set in stubborn hostility. His anger was directed at himself for his behaviour and allowing the other man to get the upper hand, something he wasn't used to. He forced himself to breathe deeply to calm his anger.

"Well, you made a right mess of that didn't you?" said Belinda, "Did you think he was going to break down and confess to a crime just because you accused him? Talk about a bull in a china shop. And why are you in such a bad mood?"

Mark remained silent. Belinda snorted.

"Oh alright, go ahead and sulk." She shook her head in frustration. They passed under West Gate in silence and Mark pulled the car over to the kerb.

"I think I've had enough of your young student friend, so I'll give Evensong a miss, if you don't mind," said Mark through tight lips. Belinda looked at him in amazement. His behaviour was very odd. Without a word she got out of the car. Mark drove off immediately. As she watched him go Belinda wondered what on earth was worrying Mark. He hadn't been his usual calm self since he arrived. Something was wrong, but what could it be? She mulled over possible causes as she turned and made her way in the late afternoon gloom, along St Peter's Street towards the Cathedral and the appointment with Tommy. No matter what Mark thought, she was keen to hear what he had to say about St Thomas's bones.

Belinda slipped in through the Cathedral's South West entrance and into the Nave. Evensong had begun in the Quire and was well attended due to the Christmas season.

"Disperse the gloomy clouds of night, and death's dark shadows put to flight. Rejoice, Rejoice, Emmanuel."

The voices of the choir rang through the ancient building. Belinda made her way along the north aisle, passing the countless memorials to souls claiming sanctuary within the consecrated walls, until she came to the Martyrdom North West transept and waited there by the Altar of the Sword's Point.

The area was shadowy with only the reflected light from the body of the church to illuminate the mystical space. As her eyes became accustomed to the spine-chilling gloom she saw two tombs opposite her. Belinda gave a shiver of fear but reminded herself that she was only a few steps away from the crowded Quire should anything happen. But what could happen?

As she waited in the iciness and dimness of the Martyrdom her memory of St Thomas's murder, a tale she'd heard many times, overwhelmed her and gradually her mind conjured up the horrific event that had happened on the spot where she stood.

"Make safe the way that leads on high, and close the path to misery. Rejoice, Rejoice, Emmanuel, Shall come to thee, O Israel."

The hymn created a hypnotic atmosphere and Belinda felt herself drifting into a dreamlike state. The centuries fell away and it seemed to her she'd become a witness to the slaughter on that fateful day in December 1170.

The knights had entered the Cathedral.

The stimulus of the moment left Reginald FitzUrse breathless and he gulped air into his lungs. Sweat trickled down his face. He looked surprised at the ease in which the attack had taken place. He had expected more resistance. Now, with the man before him reeling from the blow of his sword, his only thought was to flee to safety. But where? He glanced towards the Quire where the white faces of the now silent assembly of monks looked on in horror. Witnesses! If only the fool hadn't resisted their attempt to drag him away to the cloisters. Here, under the gaze of the Holy Virgin and all the Saints, this was sacred ground. He mouthed a desperate silent prayer.

Hugh de Moreville, not caring for his own soul, swung his great sword high and brought it down on the man's head. The man swayed, as William de Tracy also brought his sword down and, under such violence, the victim fell on all fours before his attackers. Richard le Breton stood a little apart from his colleagues, ready to mortally deter any bystander foolish enough to intervene.

The heavy metallic clang of the great swords rang through the building. A final sword blow of such force as to break the sword against the stone floor sliced through the crown of the man's head severing it from his skull.

Hugh de Moreville's clerk, who gloatingly had watched the murder, rushed forward eager to engage in the confrontation. His foot stamped on the now corpse's neck, again and again, and he gave a hideous cry of glee as brains and blood spilled over the cold stone floor.

The knights, panting from their evil accomplishment, moved towards the cloister door. Only Reginald FitzUrse lingered, gazing in mounting horror at the body at his feet. A movement in the darkness caught his eye and he saw the shadowy figure of a monk tentatively edging towards the corpse. The monk clutched at his bleeding arm and it occurred to the knight that this man had been wounded in the attack. Still the knight lingered almost unable to move. He felt a tug at his arm and heard a voice say: "Away. Let us away, He'll rise no more."

The clanking armour of his departing associates brought him to his senses and he fell back against the door, made the sign of the cross in a futile attempt to absolve himself of his crime, and staggered into the cold December evening.

The monk hurried to the corpse and knelt beside it, Vespers forgotten in the presence of unbelievable horror. Behind him he could hear the sound of his fellow monks quietly beginning to approach, the gentle slap of leather sandals on the stone stairs somehow comforting in the eerie hush. Tears flowed down his cheeks and he caressed the outstretched lifeless arm that had given him blessing.

He tore a piece from the sleeve of his habit and gently, reverently, bent in homage and began to soak up the blood flowing from the wounds and the open skull. He tried to offer a prayer but could only mutter a hoarse, "Thomas!"

Silently, a hand slid from the shadows and clutched Belinda's shoulder. A scream was stifled in her throat as another hand was placed tightly over her mouth. A guttural voice whispered in her ear: "Gottcha".

The choir concluded the carol and the Dean began a reading from the Psalms.

In a mixture of fear and rage, her heart beating wildly, Belinda broke free to see Tommy, hands clasped over his mouth and trembling in self-satisfied silent laughter. She hit out at him but he gripped her hand and, grinning, put his finger to his lips to shush her. She bit it. Tommy gave a yelp as Belinda began to pull away from him but he tightened his grip and dragged her towards worn stone steps that led down into a frightening black void.

"Where are we going?"

Tommy, ignoring the sanctity of his surrounds sang softly and mischievously: "Dem bones, dem bones, gonna walk aroun' Dem bones, dem dry bones, gonna walk aroun'. Now hear the word of the Lord."

"Yes, well, I'm in the mood to break a few," muttered Belinda.

As they descended the shadows intensified, Belinda stumbled, clung to Tommy to prevent herself from falling and cursed him under her breath in a most unchristian manner. Eventually they reached a point where Belinda was utterly immersed in an impenetrable blackness that seemed to swallow her up.

Tommy released his grip and stepped away from her. Panic rose in Belinda's chest as the pitch black weighed down on her. She gave a whimper of fear as her outstretched arms sought some form of security.

"Tommy, you idiot. Where are you?"

It was then that a beam of light shot through the darkness. Belinda blinked in the sudden light and saw illuminated before her the face of the Virgin.

Tommy had turned on a torch.

"It's Our Lady of the Undercroft," he said, a curious reverence in his voice. The white stone of the altar surrounding the Madonna glowed bright in the torch light and Belinda glimpsed a wonderful display above her of early Norman vaulting, supported by robust columns, with carved Romanesque capitals crowning each pillar.

Normally her inbuilt inquisitiveness would have demanded details about the Undercroft along with the ins and outs and associated historical minutiae but given the circumstances she decided to forgo that pleasure besides, before she had time to ask a question Tommy took hold of her arm and guided her through the darkness. The pool of torchlight settled on the floor of the crypt where a rectangular surface area had been disturbed and resealed.

"St Thomas was first buried here in the crypt and his tomb became a place of pilgrimage for those gullible enough to believe in miracles," said Tommy in a flippant manner. "And of course where there was a miracle there was money to be made, so fifty years later his remains were upgraded to the Four Star Trinity Chapel above and placed in an over-the-top memorial covered in gold and jewels, sufficient enough to dazzle the pilgrims into handing over their money."

"Destroyed by Henry. Thomas's remains were to be burned," said Belinda.

"Oooh, aren't you the little scholar," said Tommy mockingly. "But you're right. Problem was, and is, were the bones destroyed? In 1888 some historian was fixated with the idea of discovering the Norman foundations of the building and during a search on this spot, surprise, surprise, what do you think? What should pop up but a stone coffin containing the skull and bones of a man estimated to be fifty years of age at death and over six feet tall."

"Were they Thomas's?" said Belinda, her nervousness gone as she absorbed Tommy's account and felt thrilled to be so close to the site of the actual events.

"Well, Thomas was about fifty when he copped it and was supposed to be over six feet. The skull certainly had a fracture on the left side. So the bones were examined and after much 'hoo-ha', about two weeks later, were packed back in the box in the belief, by some, that they were Thomas's."

"But if it was thought …"

Tommy shushed her to be quiet. "And then in 1920 the coffin was dug up again and the bones re-examined a second time. This time it was even more strongly believed that they were Thomas's bones but again they were reburied."

"Hardly letting him rest in peace. But if it was believed they were his, why didn't they test them?"

Tommy ignored her interruption and went on: "Nearly thirty years later they were dug up yet again and this time the bones were sent to London and examined by a Professor. He was a Catholic and …"

"Don't tell me, I can guess." Belinda glanced down at the tomb's surface, so plain with nothing to identify it as a burial place. "They suspected that he would confirm the remains as being those of the great Catholic saint, and what's more in the …"

"Yes, in the Mother Church of the Anglican Communion. I can see you're a student of theological ill will," said Tommy cynically, "but after two years study to everyone's surprise he confirmed that the damage to the skull had been made by a shovel and not by a sword. So the bones were buried yet again."

Belinda felt a wave of emotion well up in her at the thought that she may actually be standing at the Saint's resting place. She could feel Tommy's hand on her arm and reluctantly allowed him to lead her away into the darkness, the pool of torchlight flittering over the cold stone floor.

"But it doesn't end there," said Tommy. "Some years ago a local here in Canterbury claimed to know of the secret site of Thomas's grave."

Tommy led Belinda across the floor of the crypt to a tomb set in the floor, a low iron chain barrier surrounding it.

"This is the grave of Grim who was Thomas's Clerk and was witness to the murder and was wounded in the attack. As you can see, next to it is what is claimed to be an unmarked grave."

The torch light swung from the tomb onto the broken surface nearby, a surface that had clearly been excavated and resealed.

"The local who made the claim and had the story passed down to him from his family members, believes that Thomas, after Henry Eight ordered his remains to be destroyed, was secretly buried here in an unmarked grave by the monks, next to his faithful clerk."

Belinda shook her head in bewilderment.

"So no one knows if his bones are actually here in the Cathedral? If the other grave proved to be false, why don't they excavate this one to see if there's someone buried here?"

With a laugh, Tommy sang softly: "Moral of the story be, Dem bones gonna rise again. Don't leave your cores for the Lord to see. Dem bones gonna rise again."

He took her arm once more and they moved away from the tombs.

"I think I've had enough talk about Thomas for one night," he said in a low voice close to Belinda's ear, "and I don't know about you, but I find it a bit chilly down here. How'd you like to warm me up?"

The light from the torch was suddenly extinguished and Belinda felt Tommy's arm slide around her waist. She tried to push him away, but he tightened his grip.

"Tommy, let go. Grow up."

His face was close to hers.

"Come on, Belinda, you know you want to. Don't tell me you really fancy that cold fish twerp that hangs around you."

His lips sought hers and he forced a kiss on her.

Belinda struggled and broke free, grabbing the torch as she did.

She hit out and struck him on the head. He gave a yelp and as the torch flew from her hand Belinda heard it clatter to the floor and roll away. Fear and panic rose in her chest. In the total dark she could see nothing but she turned in an effort to get away from Tommy and started to run.

With a thud, she ran straight into one of the huge pillars and screamed in fright. The impact stunned her and took her breath away. She heard Tommy hoarsely calling her name but he seemed a distance away so steeling herself she pressed forward in the dark, holding her hands before her to prevent running into another obstacle.

After what seemed an eternity she saw a pale light in the distance. *The steps.* If she could reach them she would be safe as she could escape up to the nave. The light increased a little as she neared the steps. As she reached the bottom one, she looked up and froze. The eerie figure of a man was silhouetted against the faint light. He was descending towards her. Frozen to the spot she watched in terror as the figure grew closer and closer.

Suddenly she was blinded by a light. She fell back in fright. The light was painful and she covered her eyes which had grown used to the dark. Then she heard her name.

"Belinda." It was Mark. As he reached the bottom step she rushed towards him and fell into his arms.

"Oh, Mark, get me out of this hell hole," she cried, as he held her close to him.

"What happened?" said Mark, flashing his torchlight into the blackness of the crypt.

"It was Tommy!"

"What? Did he hurt you? I'll wring his bloody little neck." He moved as though to search for Tommy but it was like searching for a needle in a haystack in the intense darkness of the vast crypt and a waste of time even with the torchlight.

Belinda took his hand.

"No, I'm alright. Just leave him. Let's get out of here."

With Mark's protective arm around her they headed up into the Martyrdom and the nave. Evensong was just concluding as they stepped into the full light and the concluding words of the Psalm echoed through the Cathedral,

"But the Lord is my refuge: and my God the help of my hope. And he will render them their iniquity: and in their malice he will destroy them: the Lord our God will destroy them."

Belinda sipped her brandy and gave a shiver of pleasure as the warming liquor slipped down her throat.

"But how did you find me?"

After the chill of the Cathedral Crypt they had returned to the comfort and safety of their hotel room and Belinda was tucked up in bed, duvet and plump pillows returning warmth to her welcoming body. Mark poured a brandy for himself.

"Well, I felt foolish after just dumping you and not going with you to meet that young idiot so I decided to follow on. I'm sorry for the way I acted this afternoon."

He joined her in the bed and kissed her cheek. Belinda felt the bump on her forehead where she'd collided with the stone column.

"Yes, what got into you? I've never seen you like that before."

Mark sipped his brandy.

"Now's not the time and it's a bit complicated but I'll explain later."

Belinda gave him a questioning look but knew from old that it was best not to pressure Mark. He would tell her what was worrying him in his own good time.

"OK, you knew we were to meet Tom at the Martyrdom, but how did you know I was in the crypt?"

"I heard you yelling," said Mark with a smile.

Belinda choked on some brandy that had gone down the wrong way. When she recovered from a coughing fit, she wiped her eyes and said: "Yelling. Do you mean to say they could hear me up in the nave?"

"Well, I did, I can't speak for the choir, but they did sing a bum note just about then," said Mark smiling even wider.

Mortified, Belinda sank down into the pillows.

"I didn't realize I'd been screaming and in the Cathedral of all places."

Mark laughed, enjoying her embarrassment.

"Well, you had cause to scream."

Belinda turned to him.

"But how come you had a torch with you? You didn't know I was going to be in a pitch black crypt?"

"It was my car key ring torch."

"But a little thing like that wouldn't be that bright."

Mark ran his finger down her cheek.

"Come into the twenty-first century. It has a LED Flashlight. They're very powerful. A light emitting diode is a ..." he began enthusiastically before Belinda smiled and put a finger to his lips.

Men and their toys. "Why don't you keep it you're little secret?"

Mark set his brandy glass on the bedside table and cuddled up close to Belinda.

"So, did you actually learn anything from that little snake?"

"Yes, but I'm still confused. It's possible that St Thomas's bones are buried there but for some reason no one will confirm it. And if they are, then what is it that the professor was so excited about?"

But Mark had lost interest in the subject and switched off the lamp. Then Belinda lost interest in the subject and they both found themselves with something else to consider.

The last tube train had gone and the restaurant and theatre crowds, sated now with what the city could offer, had departed as well. The London populace simply transferred its activity to the sanctuary of home and hearth. The icy streets were now deserted except for Miss Mowbray as she hurried through Eton Square, her sensible shoes echoing her presence in the early hour. There had been reports of squatters taking up residence in some of the surrounding mansions and the prospect of running into those she considered hoi polloi added to her nervousness. She had been foolish and lingered far too long in Kensington indulging in nostalgic visits to old haunts and now faced the solitary ordeal of walking the silent streets in foreign and uncertain surroundings.

Truth to tell, Miss Mowbray had also wanted time to think. After her meetings with the publishers there was much to mull over. The hotel in Ebury Street was snug but limited in comfort and her cramped room certainly not ideal for reflection on urgent matters. She'd felt the need to clear her head and the chill night air had done that but for all her deliberation she still hadn't reached a decision that was satisfactory to her.

Once or twice a young couple, arms entwined, ran giggling past her, casting amused looks at the strange old lady out alone at night, but more enchanted with each other than the concerns of others.

With some relief she turned into Ebury Street and saw in the distance the faint light above the door of her hotel. She quickened her pace.

Gradually she became aware of footsteps behind her. Not daring to look she moved faster and then broke into a faltering run. To her horror the following footsteps echoed hers and drew closer. The uneven pavement caused her to stumble but with an effort she righted herself and clung to a lamp post. A glance over her shoulder revealed a shadowy form drawing nearer and nearer.

Her chest tight with fear and gasping for breath Miss Mowbray turned away and stumbled on, straining every fibre of her being in the effort. Surely she would reach the hotel door at any moment.

Surely she would outrun her assailant.

Surely she would be safe.

Surely ...

Chapter Five

The next day saw Belinda and Hazel back at the Manor House and painstakingly carrying out the task of recording and pricing the contents. Mrs Day was away visiting her sister in Rye so apart from Mrs Jones in her province in the kitchen they had the house to themselves. Mrs Jones had brought their lunch to them and it was the first chance that Belinda had to chat with the woman. Not that there was much chat.

Mrs Jones was a small thin woman who looked as though she bore the weight of the world on her shoulders. She'd obviously been told as a child she should be seen and not heard and had carried this philosophy into her adult life. Stooped from years spent in drudgery it was almost impossible to judge her age and the shapeless rather grubby smock she wore covered up any potential clues. Her mousy hair was tied at the back of her head in what could loosely be described as a bun while her watery eyes conveyed an impression of total disinterest in the world around her. With some reluctance she answered most of Belinda's questions and it was revealed that her husband had left her years ago, she lived in the nearby housing development, didn't have the luxury of a car, even less a bicycle, and walked to and from the Manor each day to perform her duties 'below stairs' as she put it. Apart from the television soaps, which she was addicted to, her only concerns in life were her cat, Tibby and her son, Peter.

So it was coincidental that Peter's name should come up in conversation later that afternoon. Mark had returned from a day visit to Hastings where he had been showing a potential buyer a country estate for which he was managing the sale. He scooped Belinda and Hazel up from their labours, an easy task as apart from being weary, they were frozen from the cold and Hazel at least was mindful that she had still not fully recovered from her recent infection. A quick trip into the town soon had them ensconced in Mark's preferred tea shop awaiting a plate of his favourite cakes, Maid of Honour Tarts.

No sooner had they settled at their table than the door opened and the two women from the gift shop entered. Now without the green and red elf hats, they were laden with parcels and swathed in layer upon layer of heavy winter clothing so that their bulk had increased to an alarming degree. As they sighted Belinda and Mark they gave cries of glee.

"G'day. Our little Australian friend," they exclaimed in misguided attempts at an Australian accent – which only succeeded in them sounding like cockney costermongers whose barrows had just run over and crushed their feet – before erupting into a torrent of chatter as they removed several layers of their apparel and managed with some difficulty to squeeze into a limited space to seat themselves at a table nearby.

Hazel viewed them from under apprehensive eyebrows. Her need now for a gin and tonic was pressing and the proffered tea, while warm and welcoming, did little to encourage the spirit of Christmas within her. Two eccentric babbling females she did not need.

Introductions were made and if the women were aware of Hazel's displeasure they did not acknowledge it.

"I'm Molly," said the one given to romance, "and this is Peggy."

Hazel thought Tweedledum and Tweedledee more apt.

Molly leaned closer to Belinda and looked at Mark.

"Has he proposed yet?"

Twinkling eyes demanded an answer.

Belinda glanced at Mark.

"As a matter of fact, he has."

Molly clapped her hands in delight.

"I knew it. And?" she added expectantly.

Mark decided that silence was the better part of valour and retreated into a masculine shell awaiting the Maids of Honour.

Peggy broke in and touched Belinda's arm.

"Pay no attention to her dear, she's always sticking her nose into other people's business. Are you still working at the Manor House?" she said, ignoring the fact she was as guilty as her friend.

"Yes, we'll be there for a time. There is so much to do."

Hazel was about to say something but Molly claimed the floor. "And Miss Muriel Mowbray? How do you get on with her?"

This time Hazel was determined to put these lunatics in their place.

"We get along very well," she said haughtily, "not that it has anything to do with you, I'm sure."

Molly and Peggy looked at her as though questioning her sanity. Of course it had something to do with them, as did any activity in Canterbury. They switched their attention back to Belinda who seemed more fertile soil.

"We just wondered," said Peggy, "because she has the reputation of being difficult."

"Difficult?" said Molly, "more like down right rude."

Peggy nodded in agreement. "You're so right, dear. Rude. No other word for it."

"The way she treats that poor Mrs Jones is a disgrace," Molly added.

"And Mrs Day," Peggy reminded her.

Molly wrinkled her nose in disagreement.

"No. Sophia Day can look after herself. Water off a duck's back to her. But Mrs Jones is one of nature's natural victims."

"Victim, yes," confirmed Peggy sagely, "Muriel Mowbray is a right cow."

"A real scold," said Molly with conviction, "it's a pity we don't still have a ducking stool."

There was a pause in the tirade but only briefly. Sensing they would get no further with pursuing this line of questioning, Peggy enquired: "Have you had a chance to see the sights in Canterbury, or has Muriel been working you into the ground as she does with everyone else?'

"Yes, a little. We've been in the Cathedral."

The two women threw up their hands in unison.

"Oh, the Cathedral." said Molly.

"We know all about the Cathedral," added Peggy, "we used to be Holy Dusters."

This was too much for Hazel who up until now had listened to their nattering in stunned silence.

"You used to be what?" she said, in the firm belief that her original analysis of their mental instability had been confirmed.

Sensing that they had finally captured Hazel's attention the two women smiled condescendingly at her.

"Holy Dusters," they said in harmony.

"We helped the Vesturer's department clean the cathedral," continued Molly.

"Dust and polish, that sort of thing," added Peggy, "but we gave it up to work in our gift shop. Mrs Jones was a Holy Duster at one time. That's where we met her, poor soul."

Molly nodded in agreement.

"Her life's a trial, what with her husband walking out on her, leaving her to raise her son on her own."

"And he's no help to her," said Peggy, searching in her sleeve for a handkerchief, "mad as a hatter, if you ask me." She located her handkerchief and blew her nose loudly.

"You would have seen him at the Manor, no doubt," said Molly, "all dolled up like something out of a vampire movie."

"No," said Belinda, "is it Peter we're talking about? Peter Jones?"

"That's him. Tall streak of misery," said Molly, "funny clothes and a decrepit top hat. I ask you? Who'd wear a top hat these days?"

Belinda turned to Mark. "Burke and Hare. Remember we saw him at the undertakers on Sunday."

"That'd be him," sniffed Peggy, wiping her nose and filing away the information that they'd been visiting the undertaker. There had to be a story behind *that* detail. "He does odd jobs for Mr Taylor."

"Is he planning to be a funeral director?" said Mark.

Molly gave him a simpering smile. "Lord no, he does that for pocket money. No, he wants to be an archivist at the Cathedral. Where they keep all the historical records and such like."

"Manuscripts and bits of old buildings, glass and bones. Anything historical they can lay their hands on," said Peggy. "He's always hanging around the archive staff annoying them, but it won't do him any good."

"No qualifications," Molly said, with a hint of superiority.

"Does he study?" asked Belinda.

"Oh yes, but he'll never qualify." Molly tapped the side of her head. "Doesn't have it up here for that sort of job."

"That's why he was always out at the Manor House hanging around Professor de Gray, getting under his feet all the time," said Peggy. "Ever since he heard the Professor was writing his book on St Thomas, he made a nuisance of himself."

"The Professor took pity on him and gave him things to do. Nothing important I gather, but it kept Peter happy and out from under the Professor's feet," said Molly, finally tiring of the subject and running an experienced eye over the menu.

"So he would have known what the Professor had written?" said Belinda.

"Oh yes," said Peggy. "He talked of nothing else."

She glanced at the menu as Molly handed it to her.

"Do you know, I think I fancy the Spotted Dick."

Miss Mowbray's head ached. But then, so did most of her body. She found it difficult to stay conscious and every now and then drifted off. She was vaguely aware she was in a hospital and they had done something to her arm. It felt heavy and numb. If only she could remember what had happened. Blackness swamped her again and she lay immobile.

It was later. Some vague noise brought her back to consciousness. Her head felt tight as though some restricting binding was crushing it. London. She'd been in London. Why? Something to do with Walter. She'd been with him at the Victoria & Albert Museum and they had been admiring a Becket reliquary …

But Walter was dead. It must have been a dream. A memory?

Various thoughts flashed through her mind fighting for supremacy.

Someone called 'Oliver'. Sir Justin Oliver, the publisher. Why had she thought of him? He'd been at the House talking to Walter about his book.

Yes. Now she remembered. He'd been very polite, such a distinguished man, but business was business. She'd gone to London to negotiate a fee with him to publish Walter's book on St Thomas Becket.

Why hadn't she accepted his offer? It was a large amount, but perhaps she could do better? Walter wouldn't want her to accept the first offer; he'd be very upset if she did that. He'd …

But Walter was dead. She knew that only too well, and they couldn't publish without the final chapter.

There was another man, much younger. Crude. Showy. Foul-mouthed.

South Kensington. Dear old South Kensington. That's where he was. Trade? No, Trad Press. Quentin someone. He was a publisher too. Wanted Walter's book. What was it he said? Something about 'getting his own way'?

There'd been an argument and … and then she was in a dark street and someone was following her. She'd tried to get away but her brain had exploded in a flash of pain and she was falling …

Her head ached and she slowly opened her eyes, blinking in the bright light.

A young doctor stood by her. He smiled.

"How are you feeling?" Miss Mowbray slowly moved her eyes to the youthful policeman at the foot of the bed. "She appears to have been hit from behind with a large knife or machete, or so the attending police reported," she heard the doctor say, "and suffered a compound fracture. A section of her scalp was sliced away in the attack and after surgery, it required extensive stitching. She had no identification on her when she was admitted and with the head wound there is a degree of memory loss."

Mrs Jones let herself into her cottage. Well, she called it a cottage, but in reality she knew it was nothing more than another cramped 'modern commuter dwelling' as her neighbours liked to call their residences. She dropped the shopping bag onto the kitchen table, sat down and kicked off her wet shoes. The bus had been crowded and she'd had to stand most of the way home.

She wondered why Miss Mowbray had gone to London. Mrs Day didn't seem to know. It seemed a strange thing to do. She knew Muriel Mowbray hated the big city even for a day visit, yet here she was staying on and no one knew where she was staying, or what she was doing. She wondered if Peter knew anything. Tibby, her cat sniffed at the wet shoes.

"Dinner in a minute, baby," cooed Mrs Jones.

And how long was she going to be required preparing lunch for those two women. What were they doing in the house anyway? Mrs Day said they were pricing all the furniture and fittings. She felt Muriel was up to something and she didn't like it one bit.

Peter hadn't answered her call as she came through the door, which meant he was still out. It was getting late and she didn't like him wandering the streets at night. Not tonight in particular as it was Christmas Eve and they usually decorated the Christmas tree together. The old plastic one that they'd had since Peter was a boy. It would do for one more Christmas and then she'd buy a new one. Would she? Probably not. Christmas wasn't the same now that Peter had grown up.

She sighed as she unpacked her shopping bag. A tin of ham, a tinned Christmas pudding. If only Peter could get the job at the Cathedral Archives they'd have more money and maybe buy a real ham. Even a turkey. If only …

Christmas morning dawned white with snow, followed by deafening pronouncements as Cathedral bells made known the birth of Christ. With only a short distance from their hotel to the Cathedral Belinda and Mark made their way through the snow and attended the Sung Eucharist. Hazel, pleading her poor health, stayed in her warm, cozy bed but feelings of guilt plagued her and with a great display of personal sacrifice, did attend the Choral Evensong, which to her surprise lifted her spirits and upon her return to the hotel she was viewing the world if not through rose-coloured glasses at least with a modicum of good will and robust humour. The three gathered in the lounge prior to their Christmas dinner and enjoyed a champagne cocktail in honour of the festive occasion.

"So tell me about this young lout who made a pass at you in the crypt," said Hazel, nibbling on a canapé.

"Tommy?" said Belinda, "oh, he's harmless."

"You didn't think so at the time,' said Mark gruffly, "and lout is too good a word to describe him. I can think of a more accurate name."

"I'm sure you could. But you tell me that he'd been helping the Professor with his research," said Hazel turning to Belinda, "and that you found him searching his computer."

Belinda nodded.

"Well, it seems to me that he's our chief suspect," continued Hazel as she sipped her champagne."

"Murderous little bastard," said Mark.

Belinda reached for a canapé and looked at him.

"You only say that because you don't like him. But I do agree that out of the people we suspect of having something to do with the Professor's death, he seems the most likely."

Mark leaned forward.

"I admit I don't like him, but it's too early to jump to any conclusion. Remember we didn't get a satisfactory answer from the doctor or the undertaker."

"No thanks to you," said Belinda with a smile.

Mark was irked at the reminder of his unsuccessful meeting with the funeral director.

"Well, putting that aside, I'm sure they know more than they're letting on, and we still haven't followed up on the publishers."

Belinda was silent for a moment. "What was the name of that village in Bedfordshire?"

"What village in Bedfordshire?" said Hazel.

"Tommy mentioned it. Apparently the Professor went there often."

"Flaxton," said Mark, "no, Flitton."

Hazel looked at them both.

"And what's so special about Flitton?"

"There's a church there that has a mausoleum nearby, early seventeenth century or around then. It appears that generations of the de Grey family are buried there and Professor de Gray liked to think of them as his ancestors, but apparently that isn't the case," said Mark.

"Which makes me wonder if there is any connection between Flitton and the Professor's book," said Belinda.

"Now there's a thought," said Mark excitedly, "and what about that other place he visited? A nearby priory?"

"Bushmead Priory," said Belinda, catching Mark's enthusiasm, "and didn't Tommy mention that the Professor had worked on an archaeological dig there and found some bones and other things?"

Mark considered this. "Yes, but from memory that was years ago, when the Prof was a young man. I don't see how it would have any connection with his book on St Thomas."

Belinda's enthusiasm waned when she reflected on what Mark had said.

"Still, if it meant a lot to the Professor, I'd like to see the mausoleum and the Priory."

From her tone, Mark took this to be an order and knew that she would have her way. Hazel finished her champagne and searched her mind for an excuse not to go gadding about all over Bedfordshire in the middle of winter.

The week following was taken up with the continuing assessment of the contents at the Manor House. Mark returned to Bath with the promise that he would return for the New Year celebrations, which he did only to find that Hazel had gone to London to spend time with a male friend who was visiting from the United States, so Belinda and he celebrated the New Year quietly and enjoying their time alone together.

They watched a firework display and on the first day of the new year, as the weather had improved and weak sunshine filtered down from misty clouds, they visited Greyfriars Chapel. It was normally closed for the winter but Mark used his connections to enable them to have a private visit and they had the Chapel to themselves. The 13th century building straddling the River Stour enchanted Belinda and she marvelled at the remains of the Franciscan dwelling from the lifetime of St Francis and admired the unpretentious beauty of the Chapel. There was something about the building that seemed familiar to Belinda and it was only as they turned to go back to the main street that she remembered where she had seen it before.

"It's in a photo of the Professor and Miss Mowbray taken years ago," she told Mark. "I saw it on the dresser in Miss Mowbray's room." She pointed at a stone wall. "That's where he was sitting and she was standing beside him, with the Chapel in the background." She wondered what their relationship had been at that time and hoped that it had been a happy one.

As they turned into Stour Street, Mark grabbed Belinda's arm.

"There's that little snake."

Belinda looked and just caught a glimpse of Tommy as he disappeared around a corner.

"What's he doing out here?" said Belinda.

"Spying on us is my guess," said Mark as he put his arm around her. When they reached High Street there was no sign of Tommy but Belinda felt uncomfortable with the suggestion that he was following and spying on them. But why?

The next day Belinda resumed work. A telephone call from Hazel advised her that she would not be returning from London until the next day.

That means the US visitor was making certain Hazel was having a Happy New Year, thought Belinda with a smile. Mark had returned home to attend to business matters, Mrs Day was still on her holiday break and Belinda was alone in the house except for Mrs Jones, who supplied Belinda with her lunch but little else. She remained as distant as ever and as soon as she had cleared the luncheon dishes she scurried off, no doubt to her TV soaps and her cat.

The desk telephone rang in the parlour as Belinda was preparing to leave for the night. She had just switched off her laptop and was struggling into her heavy coat before facing the wintry evening and questioned who would be calling on that number. If it was for her, the caller would use her mobile number.

"Hello," said Belinda, wondering if at last it was Miss Mowbray calling to announce her return.

"This is Inspector Parks, Victoria Police Station, London," said a deep male voice. "Whom am I speaking to?"

"I'm Belinda Lawrence," said Belinda anxiously. Had something happened to Hazel? Mark?

"Are you a resident there?"

"No, I'm just working here at the moment. What's this about?"

"Do you know a Miss Muriel Mowbray?"

Belinda gave a short sigh of relief. Mark and Hazel were all right. "Yes. Miss Mowbray is employing me. Is anything the matter?"

"Is there anyone else there, a family member or relation?" said Inspector Parks.

"As far as I know Miss Mowbray doesn't have a family or any relations," said Belinda. "Has something happened to her?"

"Miss Mowbray is in hospital after a street attack and had lost her memory. The hotel where she was staying notified us when she hadn't returned there but had left her belongings. They were able to identify her. Are you absolutely sure that she has no family?"

"I can't be totally sure, but I don't think so. Why?"

The Inspector paused a moment. "Well, we are concerned because she keeps muttering the word 'rock'."

Chapter Six

Miss Mowbray stared at them with unseeing eyes. At Belinda's request Mark had driven to Canterbury, collected her and they had driven on to London where they joined Inspector Parks at the London Hospital, and other than verifying that the woman in the bed was indeed Miss Mowbray they had learned little else. The Inspector confirmed that Miss Mowbray had been found in Ebury Street unconscious and bleeding from a serious head wound. Other than the hotel proprietor's identification the police had been unable to discover anything else about her or find any motive for the attack. Belinda looked at the woman as she lay staring vacantly into space, an array of tubes and medical apparatus surrounding her, a strong woman now frail and suddenly powerless.

"She has a depressed fracture," said the doctor, "and a broken arm. With the skull, bacteria can enter through fractures like this and cause infection. Pieces of the fractured skull bone were pressing inward and there's some damage to the brain. To prevent abscesses forming we've removed foreign matter and dead tissue. The skull fragments are back in position and the wound has been stitched."

A vase of flowers on the bedside cabinet caught Belinda's eye but before she could comment on it they were moved on as a nurse came in to attend to her patient.

"That's where I was hoping you could help us," said the Inspector as they left the ward and walked down the hallway past hard-working nurses and doctors busily engaged in their healing work. "For the moment, as you seem to be the only people who know her, can you tell us what she was doing in London?"

"Well, we hardly know her," said Belinda, and explained how she and Hazel had been employed by Miss Mowbray. She handed the Inspector a business card. "This is her solicitor's address. So you see we can't really help, except that we can make a guess as to why she was here in London."

"And that is?" asked the Inspector.

Belinda explained further about the Professor's book and the two publishers who were vying to obtain publishing rights.

"And you think she had meetings with these two?" said Inspector Parks. "Do you know who they are?"

"I can help you there," said Mark, as he reached into his pocket for his mobile address book.

He gave the details to the Inspector, who duly noted them down.

"I'll have our men get onto tracking down her solicitor in Canterbury." He looked at the business card. "Fosdyke? Perhaps he can tell us if she has a family or any children. And what about this 'rock' she keeps asking for? Any thoughts on that?"

Belinda and Mark looked at each other.

"I'm afraid we can't help you there," said Mark. Belinda nodded agreement. "We know very little about Miss Mowbray, only that we assumed she hadn't been married."

The Inspector cleared his throat.

"That doesn't seem to be an impediment these days to having children. And of course at her age …" He gave a hopeless gesture. "But it could be that she'd had a brother at some time and that was his knick name. He might have died and in her current condition, she could be mourning for him. On the other hand, it might just be wild ramblings due to her troubled mind. Perhaps she had a rock collection as a child."

Belinda looked at him in amazement. "Pardon?"

"Well, people do you know, and with her mind disturbed, well, maybe she's just romancing. Maybe it means nothing at all. It was a particularly vicious attack and the doctors say it'll be some time before she fully recovers, if she does." The Inspector turned to them as they reached the front door. "You have my contact details. If you do remember anything or discover anything that can help us, let me know." With that he walked swiftly away. Belinda and Mark stood for a moment in the hospital foyer.

"Rock collection?" said Mark, with a laugh, "what was he on about?"

Belinda smiled.

"What now? Back to Canterbury?"

Mark looked at his watch.

"St Martin's Lane is one of my favourite streets in London."

Belinda looked at him in disbelief.

"What on earth are you talking about?"

"Theatreland. The Duke of York's theatre, where Peter Pan was first performed."

"Are you mad? What are you on about?" asked Belinda, fearing that Mark had lost the plot. It was hardly the time to go sightseeing.

"It's also where Sir Justin Oliver, of Oliver & Oliver Inc. Publishers, has his office." Mark took her arm and guided her out into the street. "And I think it's about time we paid him a visit, don't you?"

Sir Justin Oliver reminded Belinda less of Peter Pan and more of a garden gnome. An inflated garden gnome who reeked of Savile Row. White hair topped his ruddy face and sociable smile. He sat behind his vast desk beaming at his visitors and with podgy fingers snapped highly elaborate trouser braces against his navy and white broad-striped shirt. A colourful bow tie threatened to vanish beneath his baby pink jowls.

"Dear Miss Mowbray." He chuckled. "Quite an innocent in many ways. And you say she was attacked in the street?" His manner suddenly changed from being light-hearted to intense seriousness. "Streets aren't safe you know. England's changed you know." He leaned across the desk, "And not for the better, I can assure you," he added conspiratorially. Having thus stated his opinion on the state of the country he sat back in his chair and viewed his visitors with a guarded eye.

"So Miss Mowbray did visit you?" said Belinda.

Sir Justin engaged his thumbs behind his braces and snapped them once more.

"I can't deny it. She did. I'd had preliminary discussions with the late Professor de Gray regarding the possibility of publishing his new book, but to be frank, nothing he had shown me contained any new material relating to St Thomas."

"The Professor claimed he had a new discovery that was sensational," said Mark.

"True," admitted Sir Justin, looking Mark in the eye. "I tried to convince him to let me read the details in the final chapter so that I could make a judgement on whether to publish or not, but he wouldn't reveal that sensational news until we had agreed to publish. Well, I ask you? Would you buy a pig in a poke?" He shook his jowls in affronted confirmation of what he considered a poor business proposition. "No, and neither would I."

"Did you visit him in Canterbury?"

"Once."

"When was that?"

"Oh, let me see. Early in the year, from memory."

"You didn't visit again, say just before he died?"

Sir Justin gave a world-weary smile.

"What would have been the point?"

"Where you surprised when he died so suddenly?"

"Not really, he was getting on a bit."

"So you didn't see him any other time?"

"Only here in London when he first offered the book to me."

"Did Miss Mowbray offer you the manuscript?" said Mark.

"She did. I think she wanted it to be published in his memory but like the Professor she wanted a publishing contract before she revealed the last chapter, which she assures me contains the information the late Professor felt was exciting, and which I gather is in her possession."

"She said that?" said Belinda.

"That's what the lady led me to believe."

"And you rejected her?"

"My dear, how could I accept? Furthermore, she demanded a highly fanciful sum of money for the rights. Books of this type have a limited market, mostly academic, and are published more for a prestigious return than a monetary one."

"You know that there was another publisher interested in the book," said Mark.

Sir Justin gave a loud guffaw.

"Publisher? You mean young Frazer, I suppose. A jumped up Johnny-come-lately, thinks he knows all there is to know. Yes, I'd heard that the Professor had discussions with him and it seems he was more willing to play ball. But even he wouldn't be so stupid as to enter into a contract without seeing all the manuscript."

"Why do you think the Professor was so keen to keep what he'd discovered so secret?" said Belinda.

Sir Justin shrugged his broad shoulders.

"Who knows? If indeed he had discovered some vital new details about St Thomas he may have felt it was too precious to reveal until he knew he had a publisher, in case it fell into other less conscientious hands."

"Couldn't he have just published a paper on it?" said Mark.

"Yes, he could have, but maybe he believed it was sensational enough to earn him his fortune and putting it out there before the public with all the attendant publicity was the way to do it. Foolish of course, for as I said, a limited market."

"And Miss Mowbray wants to do the same?"

"It appears so, but without her handing over the final chapter, I'm afraid it's not going to happen."

Feeling that they would get no further information from Sir Justin, Belinda and Mark bade him good-day and left the office.

As the door closed behind them Sir Justin drummed his fingers on the desk top as he thought over the recent conversation. He reached for the intercom switch.

"Miss Barden, get onto the hospital and make sure I'm kept up to date on Miss Mowbray's condition. Oh, and send her some more flowers."

"Yes, Sir Justin, and there's a Police Inspector Parks wishing to see you. Shall I send him in?"

Hazel closed the door of the Manor House behind her. She knew that Mrs Day was still away and Mrs Jones would have long gone, if she had been at the house at all that day. Belinda had telephoned her in London and told her of the attack on Miss Mowbray and that she and Mark were going to the hospital. Hazel had no intention of visiting the hospital. She had a long standing fear of doctors and medical conditions and kept them at arm's length. As her American friend had returned home, she'd driven straight to Canterbury with one thing on her mind and the empty house provided the ideal opportunity to carry out her plan.

She deposited her coat and bag in the parlour and crept out into the hall.

Why am I creeping about? she thought. But the silent empty house did seem threatening and she gave a shiver. However, Hazel knew she was made of sterner stuff and striding forth, shoulders back, continued on down to the empty rooms. She was convinced that clues to the missing USB file were to be found somewhere in the House, and now that she had it to herself it was the perfect time. A quick glance in each of these rooms revealed little and it was only at the bottom of the passageway that she came to the end of her search. Miss Mowbray's quarters. Belinda had mentioned them and Hazel had retained a niggling curiosity about the rooms and had been determined to inspect them.

Stepping into the bedroom Hazel took in the jumble of furniture and inhaled the fragrance of lavender and roses. She sneezed. Such sentimental perfumes always irritated her sinus. Her preference was for masculine scents, a blend of leather fragrance with a touch of citrus, wood and moss.

The bathroom revealed little but that was to be expected. No, what Hazel sought was somewhere in this room she was certain. But where?

Pulling open the top drawer of the dresser she rummaged through underwear, handkerchiefs and a few personal items. Some stockings and scarves along with old theatre programmes filled the other drawer.

The two bottom draws were full of books. Hazel pulled one out. It was a diary. The other books proved to be diaries as well, all Miss Mowbray's, dating back many years. Hazel flicked through one. 'Today I finished typing Walter's paper on Medieval Diseases: Cause and Effect'. Flicking through other books revealed similar entries.

Her diaries are dry as dust, like the writer, thought Hazel.

She packed the books back into the drawers, cursed and stood looking at the photograph as she recognized Miss Mowbray and the Professor.

"Where have you hidden it you old biddy," said Hazel, addressing the image.

With no answer forthcoming, Hazel turned her attention to the great Victorian mahogany wardrobe that rather dominated the room. Obviously intended for a larger room it reached nearly to the ceiling. The long drawer underneath revealed nothing more than some folded threadbare blankets and pillowcases. Swinging open the solid doors, Hazel found dresses and coats hanging there, plus shoes and hats but little else. Not content with this she turned her attention to the bed. Pulling off the pillowcases she pummelled each pillow in search of something solid but all she could feel was duck down.

Stripping off the blankets and sheets she ran her hands over the mattress for any sign of a foreign object. But to no avail.

On her haunches she searched under the bed but was greeted by an ornate Victorian chamber pot and quite a few balls of fluff. Clearly Mrs Day was not as thorough in her cleaning as she would have them believe. Rising, she went into the bathroom again and opened the medicine cabinet. Toothpaste and various containers of herbal pills stood in solitary rows.

Frustrated, Hazel shut the door with a bang. She glanced in the mirror and saw in it the reflection of the wardrobe. From this angle she could just see the top and the edge of something nestling there. It appeared to be the lip of a vase or container. Feeling that she might have discovered the object of her quest, and realizing that she wouldn't be able to reach up that high, she took hold of a rickety Chippendale chair and dragged it over to the wardrobe. With care she placed one stiletto heeled foot on the seat and then the other. The chair creaked ominously.

Holding herself steady against the sturdy closet she stretched up and slid one hand over the top. Her fingers fluttered around searching for contact with the object. Success. Just as she had it nearly in her grasp …

"*What in God's name are you doing?*" The shrieking voice shocked her and she lost her footing. The chair slid away from under her and she was left clinging to the wardrobe, her feet swinging freely.

Mrs Day took in the spectacle. Bed linen scattered about the room, the mattress askew, drawers open and Hazel Whitby, arms extended above her head, clinging to the top of the wardrobe and hung like a side of aged beef. One shoe slipped off her foot to plop onto the floor. Hazel turned her head to look down at Mrs Day and gave, what she hoped, was a blameless smile.

"I was looking for a cigarette."

Mr Fosdyke shuffled into the room, spectacles on the end of his nose and a bulging and rather dilapidated manila file under his arm.

Hazel, after a grilling by Mrs Day to 'please explain' her presence in Miss Mowbray's bedroom and failing dismally to provide an adequate answer, or one that satisfied the housekeeper, had fled the House to avoid any further confrontation with the woman and so seized the opportunity of calling on Mr Fosdyke, who, she knew, had been the Professor's lawyer and was still handling his estate. The lawyer lived in the small village of Fordwich a few miles out of Canterbury, an idyllic setting on the River Stour. That information she'd been able to chisel from a reluctant Mrs Day who privately regarded her now as seriously deranged.

The Oast House cottage seemed ideal for this little man, stooped and cursed with crippling arthritis, but he presented a jovial attitude towards life.

"As you can see, Mrs Whitby, I work from home now as I'm partially retired. I've kept a few clients just to keep my oar in the water, so to speak." He chuckled as he sank slowly into a leather wing chair and brushed what remained of his white hair back from his unlined forehead.

"I think I prefer Ms to Mrs these days," said Hazel, as she noticed a large ashtray nearby. *Did the lawyer smoke? Could she ask for a cigarette?*

Mr Fosdyke looked intensely interested.

"Do you really?" He sat back in his chair, his finger tips placed together, the file balanced precariously on his knees. "Generations come and generations go," he continued, slipping into a philosophical mood. "Now with *my* generation the preferred term was 'Mrs' as opposed to 'Miss', which indicated that a woman was unmarried and didn't have the support of a husband, whereas this generation …"

"Do you have a cigarette?" Hazel interrupted, a certain urgency overwhelming her. Surely she could smell the exotic remainder of cigarette smoke? The lawyer looked at her in surprise.

"A cigarette? Why no, I don't."

Hazel inched the ash tray towards him.

"I saw this and thought you may be a smoker."

Mr Fosdyke gave a low chuckle.

"Good heavens, no. I leave that out for an old friend, a man of the cloth, who smokes like a chimney. Takes me days to get rid of the disgusting smell. For myself I believe it to be a filthy habit."

Hazel gave a weak smile.

"I do so agree," she said in a feeble voice that carried not one iota of conviction.

"But you didn't come here to talk about smoking," said the lawyer as he open the file and rummaged through the contents.

"No, I wanted your advice on my situation now that Miss Mowbray is hospitalised," replied Hazel.

"The police have not long been in contact with me and the hospital said they will keep me abreast of her condition," said Mr Fosdyke with a sad shake of his head. He selected a document and inspected it. "I gather that Muriel engaged you to catalogue and evaluate the contents of the Manor House. As you have an agreement and as Muriel is likely to recover, as far as we know, I see no reason for you to discontinue your work."

"What if she doesn't recover?"

The lawyer pursed his lips, took off his glasses and twirled them around with his fingers.

"Naturally, one would hope that she does recover. If indeed she does pass away, then the house contents, which she inherited from Walter, would need to be evaluated anyway, so there is no reason as I said, for you to stop doing what you're doing."

"And payment?" said Hazel somewhat anxiously.

"Be assured you will be paid in either case. I will guarantee that."

Hazel gave a nod of satisfaction and rose to go.

"Thank you, Mr Fosdyke. I appreciate your help."

The old man with great effort managed to extricate himself from his chair.

"Delighted to meet you, Mrs – Ms Whitby. Tell me, have you been to Fordwich before?"

"No, this is my first time."

"Oh, well, you can't leave without seeing our most famous attraction, the Fordwich Stone. I'll get my coat and accompany you. It's only a few steps to the old church."

Hazel's heart sank as he struggled into a bulky overcoat and put on a worn suede peaked cap with fur lined flaps that fell down covering his ears.

He looks like Elmer Fudd, she thought. She made an elaborate show of glancing at her watch hoping to deter him.

"Thank you for the offer, but I really must be getting back to Canterbury."

But Mr Fosdyke would have none of it and taking hold of two walking sticks he ushered a reluctant Hazel out into the street. Bent over and tottering along with a walking stick in each hand he resembled an infirm insect. Slowly they made their way towards St Mary's with only the shingled spire to be seen through the surrounding trees.

"I imagine you've been the Professor's lawyer for a long time," said Hazel, more for polite conversation than for any interest.

"Oh no, only the past few years," came the reply, as Mr Fosdyke winced in pain and wondered just why he had been foolish enough to suggest this outing. "No, I acted for his wife, Helen de Goderigge that was. Dear Helen had been my client for many years, in fact after my wife died, I rather thought I'd set my cap at her, but Walter was the better man. It was a tragedy when she died. To fall to her death in the house that she had inherited, as I said a tragedy. So Walter asked me to stay on as his solicitor, which I was happy to do."

"And you would have known when he changed his will?"

"Yes. He decided to offer the house to National Heritage Trust, which they accepted. Muriel was rather put out and made sure he knew her feelings on the matter. She'd wanted the house very much."

They arrived at St Mary's by the River Stour and upon entering, made their way past box pews until they reached the Fordwich Stone, a very slim rectangular limestone block of some five feet in height and covered in superb carvings.

"This is known as St Augustine's tomb," said Mr Fosdyke, with more than an element of pride in his voice. "St Augustine, as you no doubt know, brought Christianity to Britain."

Hazel stifled a yawn as he continued: "It's uncertain when it first came to Fordwich. There is no doubt it was a shrine, but is it the shrine of St Augustine?"

Hazel felt the question to be rhetorical and didn't feel called upon to offer an answer.

"Well, thank you very much for showing it to me," she said turning to go, "most interesting."

The lawyer, a little bewildered at her hasty retreat, shuffled down the aisle after her.

"Tell me, Mr Fosdyke, as you knew the Professor and Miss Mowbray so well, were you at all surprised that he was cremated so quickly?"

"To tell the truth I was a little, but Muriel Mowbray advised me that Walter had requested it. I did query this with her and she said he had written a letter indicating that it was his wish."

"Did she have a letter?"

"Yes. I requested that I be allowed to see it and she sent it over with that young man that helped out, Peter? I think that's his name."

"And was the letter signed by the Professor?"

"Yes, it looked a lot like his signature."

Hazel stopped at the church entrance.

"What do you mean, looked a lot like his signature?"

Mr Fosdyke was glad to have a chance to stop and catch his breath.

"Well, it was a bit odd. Like it but not, if you know what I mean. I rang Muriel and questioned it, but she said that Walter had been getting frail and his hands were shaking so his signature was a bit wobbly."

"Were they? His hands shaking?"

"I had to take her word for it, as I hadn't seen Walter in person for a year or more."

"Was the letter handwritten?"

"Typed with his signature below."

"So it could have been forged?"

Mr Fosdyke looked anxious.

"It could have been I suppose. But who would do that?"

Who indeed thought Hazel as she walked to her car. The lawyer trailed behind her.

"Anyway," he said, "the doctor had produced a death certificate so I could see no reason to raise an objection."

"That old bat? She's a right pain," said Quentin Frazer through thin lips and with some venom in his voice. He stood looking out of his publishing office window onto Cornwall Gardens. An aggressive twenty-five year old with a sallow complexion, dressed now in designer tattered jeans and a Jermyn Street shirt open at the neck, he played with the silver dollar that hung there on a silver chain. He turned back to Belinda and Mark who sat opposite his desk. With a toss of his head that sent his long blond hair flying, he sat down and put his feet up on the desk, displaying faux cowboy boots. Belinda decided that he had a personality problem.

"But you saw her recently?" said Mark, who could barely conceal his dislike for the man.

"Yeah, she came here rabbiting on about the book that the old Professor had written. I'd expressed interest in publishing it, even though I knew it wouldn't be a best seller." He sniggered at the thought.

"Then why make the offer?"

"Well, you know, sometimes you have to have a quality item on your list."

Mark doubted if the man would know a quality item if it bit him on the bum.

"But if it contained some sensational discovery regarding Thomas Becket there was the possibility of a best seller, surely?"

Quentin looked at him with new interest.

"So you know about that."

"Yes, and obviously so do you."

Quentin was silent for a moment.

"Yeah, well sure I knew."

"And you went to Canterbury to get the Professor to tell you what he'd discovered."

"I may have. What's it to you?"

"My guess is that it was about six months ago, just before he died, am I right?"

"Could be. Look, what's this all about?"

"It seems there's a mystery about the way the Professor died."

"I heard he had a heart attack."

"Possibly."

"Possibly? What are you suggesting? He was murdered? Over his crummy book? Don't make me laugh and don't try and lay the blame on me, mate," Quentin said angrily.

"But you're still interested in publishing this 'crummy book' as you call it."

Quentin made a laconic gesture.

"It's possible that the old boy had hit on something, something that could be a money spinner."

"And Miss Mowbray still wants it published."

"Sure, but the old bird wouldn't release the final chapter that has all the details. I pleaded with her when she was here the other day and told her no chapter, no deal, but there're ways and means of getting what I wanted. She said she'd go away and think about it. And then she got herself bashed and ended up in hospital."

Belinda sat upright.

"How do you know that?" she demanded.

Quentin look confused for a moment and then shrugged.

"I don't know. Maybe I read it in the papers or it was on TV."

"I don't think so," said Belinda tightly. "It was last night that the police knew who she was and there hasn't been any publicity."

Quentin shrugged again and gesticulated, waving one hand airily about his head.

"How the hell should I know? Maybe it was gossip in the trade. Word gets around you know."

Mark rose and leaned over the desk.

"And maybe you arranged for her to 'get bashed'. ".

Quentin took his feet off the desk and sat upright glaring pure hatred at Mark.

"Listen, college boy; don't start making accusations against me because some old duck gets mugged. I don't know who you are and I don't have to answer any of your questions. If I get to hear that you've been slandering me, then maybe you'll end up in the gutter with your head split open."

"Curtesy of one of your cronies? Maybe the one who battered the old lady?"

Quentin leapt to his feet ready for a fight but seemed to think better of it, stared at Mark for a moment and picked up the telephone and punched in a number.

"I'm busy. Just get out of my office," he snarled viciously. Ignoring them he began a conversation, "Hello darlin', did you enjoy last night? Me to. Is your old man still away?" He gave a grubby chuckle, turned his back and looked out the window.

Mark made a move towards him, but Belinda grabbed his arm.

"Let's go."

Fighting back his anger, Mark strode from the office with Belinda close behind.

Mrs Day stirred three spoons of sugar into her cup of tea. She normally never had sugar but, as she knew from bitter past experience, the quality of the tea that Mrs Jones served up was so poor that even four spoonfuls wouldn't really mask the disgusting flavour. But it would be unneighbourly to refuse and besides, she had news to hand down. The state of Mrs Jones' kitchen did nothing to inspire confidence and she surreptitiously wiped the rim of the cup before taking a cautious sip.

"All I know is that she's in hospital and seriously ill."

Mrs Jones frowned.

"Did they say what happened?"

"Well, it seems she was attacked in the street," said Mrs Day, reaching for a jam biscuit in the vain hope that it would reduce the sourness of the tea. It didn't.

Mrs Jones wrung her hands.

"I told her not to go to London. I warned her. London is such a terrible place these days. I see it on the telly news every night. "

Mrs Day looked at her in surprise.

"She told you she was going?"

"Well, why not?" said Mrs Jones defensively. "I am employed there and I do have to make lunch for those women she's got going through every room in the house."

"Every room indeed," said Mrs Day indignantly, warming to the subject. "I found one of them, the old one, swinging from the wardrobe in Muriel's room. As large as life and the room in a terrible state." Without thinking she took a vigorous gulp of tea, which worked in every way to distract her from her indignation.

"What was she doing in her room?" said Mrs Jones abruptly.

Mrs Day was on the point of regurgitating the tea but managed to recover. She put the tea cup down well out of reach lest she make the same mistake again.

"That's what I wanted to know. I didn't get a sensible answer and it took me forever to get the room cleaned up and back to normal."

"Did she say what she'd been doing in there?"

"No. Personally I think she was just having a sticky beak."

Mrs Jones looked thoughtful.

"What do you suppose will happen now?"

"About what?"

"Well, everything. If anything happens to Muriel, what will happen to the house? To us? And what about those two women, will they stay on doing whatever it is they're doing?"

Mrs Day assumed her role as housekeeper and therefore the superior employee.

"For the moment we go on as normal. I've spoken with Muriel's lawyer, Mr Fosdyke, and told him the situation. He's been in contact the London police but for now he says that we will be paid as usual and those women will complete what they are doing."

"But what happens if Muriel dies? What then?"

"We'll worry about that if and when it happens," said Mrs Day rising and picking up her handbag.

"Won't you have another cup of tea?" said Mrs Jones.

Mrs Day hurried to the door.

"Thank you, no. One was enough. So refreshing," she lied.

After her visitor was gone, Mrs Jones sat for a full twenty minutes in silence with the cat on her lap. The television was screening a children's show but it didn't impinge upon her consciousness as she was deep in thought. What if Muriel Mowbray did die? What would happen to her then? Would she still have a job? And what was that woman looking for in Muriel's room? So many questions, questions that needed answering.

"I hadn't thought about ringing Mr Fosdyke, had I Tibby?" she said suddenly, in a determined voice.

The dozing cat jumped in fright and was unceremoniously dumped on the floor. Mrs Jones reached for her telephone and dialled a number.

The wide ribbon of the M1 motorway carried Belinda and Mark away from London and into the wide green fields of Bedfordshire. Rather than return immediately to Canterbury, Belinda confided her desire to visit the village of Flitton and the de Grey memorial that had so intrigued Professor de Gray. As they left London behind them Mark's anger at the behaviour of Quentin Frazer had begun to wane, although his intense dislike of the man and his odious character still made his blood boil.

Mark slowed the car, turned off the main road and drove through a series of gentle hills and peaceful valleys dotted with small towns, wheat fields green from the autumn sowing, while pocket-sized villages displayed all the signs of an idyllic existence. A funeral departing one village church caught Belinda's eye. The hearse was covered with an abundance of flowers, riotous in their colour amid the grey of the winter light. She craned her neck around to watch as they passed by the church and then sat back in her seat with a thoughtful expression.

"Flowers."

Mark took his eyes off the road for a moment to glance at her.

"Flowers? What about flowers?

"That funeral made me think. Did you notice when we were at the hospital that there was a vase of flowers next to Miss Mowbray's bed?"

"Didn't really notice. But what of them?"

"No one knew who she was or that she was in hospital, so who would have sent her flowers."

"Maybe they were left by a previous patient."

Belinda thought this over then shook her head.

"No. They were fresh, I'm sure.

"If they'd been addressed to her, then the hospital would have known her name," said Mark.

"True, but if there was no name, just addressed 'to the woman who was bashed' or something like that."

"But the police would have been able to track down the florist and find who had ordered the flowers."

"Maybe they tried to, but the florist might not have known the person who ordered them. Anyone could have just walked in off the street and given the instructions, paid cash and walked out."

"Anyone being?"

Belinda sighed.

"That's the question. We can assume that it wasn't just someone who'd somehow heard of the bashing and felt sorry for Miss Mowbray, so it has to be someone who knew her and knew what had happened."

"And the two who knew for certain she was in London are the publishers, Sir Justin and that pathetic apology for a man, Quentin Frazer."

"I can't see him sending flowers to anyone, except some impressionable teenager whose knickers he wanted to get into. Besides, I'm more than certain he arranged the bashing. What was it he told Miss Mowbray? 'I'll get what I want'?

"'There's ways and means of getting what I wanted' were his exact words, if I remember correctly," said Mark as he turned the wheel to send the car off along another road.

"We can rule out Mrs Day," said Belinda, "because she's probably still away and doesn't know what's happened and I doubt that she'd send flowers either. No love lost there I suspect. So that leaves Sir Justin but he claims the first he'd heard of the bashing was when we told him."

"The other thing is that we only have Sir Justin's word that Miss Mowbray hadn't signed a contract with him to publish."

"But why then would she go and visit Quentin?"

"Maybe to rub it in his face. Tell him she didn't need him. After all, we only have his word as well as to what happened when she paid him a visit."

"That's true," said Belinda, "and maybe he decided to have her bashed as a payback."

"There's something else about all this that we haven't considered," said Mark.

Belinda looked at him.

"What's that?"

"Well, firstly the Professor gets hit on the head. Then Miss Mowbray gets her head bashed in. Do you see a pattern emerging?"

"Well, they both got head wounds … Oh," said Belinda as she suddenly realised what Mark meant. "So did Thomas Becket."

Any further thought or discussion on this intriguing theory was curtailed for the moment, as they had arrived at the village of Flitton. Mark turned off the main road and parked the car outside the ancient church of St John the Baptist. Having obtained the key from the key-keeper they approached the mausoleum.

The 15th century church itself stood on a slight mound and the white stucco de Grey mausoleum was located against the north side of the chancel. If Belinda thought she would discover any clues to the murder of Professor de Gray in this location she was doomed to disappointment. While the early 17th century last resting place of the family was impressive, with many of the marble figures draped in classical fashion and numerous alabaster memorials with ornate decoration of cherubs, animals, fruit, flowers and skulls, it offered nothing in the way of clues to help solve a mystery. Belinda felt rather sheepish as they walked back to the car after returning the key and spending what she considered a wasted half-hour with the dead.

"I'm sorry to have dragged you all this way for nothing," she said as she gave an awkward smile to Mark.

"Not at all. It won't be wasted. We're only a few miles from Bushmead Priory where the Professor did his archaeological dig all those years ago."

They got into the car and Mark started the engine.

"But what can we find there?" said Belinda. "There's not much of it left now, is there?"

"Nevertheless, I want to check it out. It must mean something for the Professor to have kept returning there. You got your wish to see the mausoleum, now I want to get my wish." He gave Belinda an encouraging smile and they set off once again.

On another wild goose chase, thought Belinda as she settled back and watched the countryside drift by.

It was late in the afternoon when they approached the Priory and Belinda drew her overcoat around her to ward off a sharp breeze that had sprung up. The remaining building of the Priory, the Refectory with its honey-coloured stone walls, had taken on an ethereal ambience in the dim light.

As they walked along the path for a closer inspection, a sprightly grey-haired man, hands tucked into the pockets of his anorak, appeared from around the corner of the building. He had an equally sprightly Jack Russell terrier on a lead and was obviously walking his dog before nightfall. He greeted Belinda and Mark.

"Good evening. Were you hoping to see inside the Refectory? It's not open in winter, sad to say. Have you come far?"

"Up from London," said Mark.

The man frowned as though in those few words, Mark had indicated they were lost souls.

"Pity to have wasted your time after such a long drive, and to have missed the fourteenth century wall paintings. They're a joy to behold. Maybe you'll come back in the summer."

The man began to stroll on and they walked with him. He seemed a fountain of knowledge and eager to share it.

"Only the refectory and a few bits of other buildings survive, but originally there was a church, cloister, chapter house and an infirmary. After the Reformation and over the years it was sold and the refectory and chapter house were transformed into a mansion, then there was …

"A friend of our used to come here regularly, Professor de Gray," Mark interrupted rather rudely, fearing the historical diatribe would be endless.

The man stopped and turned to look at them.

"You know Walter? How is the old rascal?"

"I'm afraid he passed away. Sorry to have to tell you."

"Passed away?" The man looked surprised. "When did this happen?"

"About six months ago," said Belinda.

The man looked at her.

"No? Really? I'm sorry to hear that. I've known him for, oh, it must be over fifty years. First met him when they were pulling down the old Georgian façade that someone was unwise enough to have added in the eighteenth century." He waved a hand towards the Refectory. "It was an opportunity to have a dig and see what we could discover, you know. I was about ten years younger than him I think, but we hit it off and stayed in contact over the years."

"The dig would have been exciting," said Belinda. "We know he was excited by it. He found some items of interest, or at least, of interest to him."

The man chuckled.

"Yes, he was quite thrilled with what he'd found. Mind you, from what I recall, it was only bits of rubbish and few coins and bones. Nothing of real value, but he seemed happy enough." The man shook his head and was silent for a moment. "Six months ago, you say? Why that couldn't have been much after he was last here."

"You saw him then?" asked Belinda.

"Yes, let me think." The man looked at the sky for inspiration. "Where are we now, January? Well, it must have been about last May or June. Yes, June it was. He'd often come up from Canterbury and we usually got together and had a pint or two, but last June he was with another fellow. He'd driven Walter up here, after his usual detour to the de Grey mausoleum. Walter seemed upset about something, not his usual self, if you know what I mean. Didn't stay long, so we really didn't get a chance to talk."

"This other chap, was he a twenty-year old student type," said Mark, "with spiky dark hair. Wore jeans?" The man shook his head. "No not him. You mean Tommy? I know Tommy. He often drove Walter up here. But this man, he was older than that. A bit odd if you ask me."

"What do you mean?"

"He was dressed in a strange way. Had on a long black coat and …" The man chuckled at the thought. "He had a top hat. Imagine that. In this day and age. Lord knows where Walter dug him up from."

Belinda and Mark exchanged a glance. *Peter Jones.*

The Jack Russell whimpered, anxious to get his walk.

"Best be off," said the man, as a faint drizzle began. He looked at the dog. "He thinks he can scent a fox that's gone to ground, but I won't disillusion him. Sorry to hear about old Walter. I'll miss him. What carried him off?"

"A heart attack – they say," said Belinda diffidently.

The man nodded sagely.

"Sad news. I was looking forward to his next visit. He told me that next time we met he would have some exciting news to tell me. Now I suppose I'll never know what it was." He made a despairing gesture and then was off, the dog straining at his lead hoping to find his imaginary fox.

As frozen rain shattered against the car windscreen, Hazel drove through the silent Canterbury streets. The citizens were all abed happily snoring and dreaming of sunny beaches while she, enclosed in her warm cocoon, glided by the last of the darkened commuter houses until murky and uninviting open fields surrounded her. The headlights of the car soon picked out the sinister shapes of the trees surrounding the Manor House. She drove up to the front of the house, stopped the car and switched off the engine. In the silent night the faint thump of the sleet on the car roof was the only sound. She peered at the house through the windscreen. The building had become an eerie monstrous shape barely visible in the darkness. An ordinary soul might have found their knees knocking and beaten a hasty retreat but Hazel Whitby was a woman on a mission. She had been forced to wait until Belinda and Mark had retired for the night before she could make her clandestine getaway to return to the house.

Her misadventure of earlier in the day, witnessed by an outraged Mrs Day, Hazel had kept to herself, partly through embarrassment and partly through a desire to solve this mystery without Belinda and Mark's help. She made her way to the front door. Pride comes before a fall, she knew only too well, but she was convinced that whatever she had discovered on top of the wardrobe in Miss Mowbray's room was of vital importance and she intended to discover its contents and eventually accept the accolades for solving the puzzle surrounding the Professor's death.

The entrance hall was almost pitch black before Hazel switched on the light. Not that it was much better then as the wiring in this part of the building was old and the globes only threw a faint light over the gloomy space. Guiding herself by placing a hand on the wall she headed down the passageway to Miss Mowbray's room. The click of the light switch and subsequent illumination revealed that Mrs Day had restored the room to its former state and no sign of Hazel's debacle remained.

With some haste she moved across the room to the Chippendale chair and once more dragged it over to the wardrobe. Once bitten twice shy, Hazel removed her high heels and with great care and trepidation she placed one foot on the chair and then the other. So far so good. But as she reached up she realised that, by removing her shoes, she was slightly shorter. This made stretching up harder than before.

With an extra effort and by standing on the tips of her toes, her hand reached the top and investigative fingers sought the desired object. Once more she was successful and managed to grasp it and edge it over the wardrobe top.

It was at this moment that the 18th century chair, made by Thomas Chippendale for purposes other than what Hazel was now subjecting it to, finally succumbed to the laws of physics and collapsed in a heap of rubble.

Hazel fell with it, but this time she brought with her a large ceramic vase. As it fell along with her, the top came off and Hazel was covered in a gritty grey residue.

She sat slightly stunned on the floor and brushed some of the dust from her face. Rubbing a little of it between her fingers, she wondered what the substance was.

Then with mounting horror she realised its origin.

She was covered in Professor de Gray.

Chapter Seven

The sickening shriek of disgust and revulsion that Hazel gave echoed into the night and convinced a lone traveller, passing some distance away, that he had heard the wail of a Banshee fresh from the Otherworld bringing forth her prophecy of death. It encouraged him not to be tardy and so increased his speed, not to mention his heart rate.

In the bedroom, Hazel continued to have hysterics as she stamped her feet in a kind of riotous tap dance around the broken urn, shook her head to clear it of the ashes and continued to screech inventive obscenities. In a frenzy of distaste she tore off her clothing and rushed to the bathroom. In the shower she lathered soap until she had used almost the entire bar, letting the warm water wash away any sign of the deceased Professor. It was a good twenty minutes before she felt cleansed and was able to turn the water off.

Drying herself on a towel she realised that she would not be able to put her ash impregnated clothes on again and didn't cherish returning to the hotel in the nude. It occurred to her that she might wear some of Miss Mowbray's clothes that she'd seen hanging in the wardrobe, but her recollection of their drabness convinced her that the naked option was the better of the two. Luckily she saw a gaudy floral dressing gown hanging on a hook behind the door and wrapped herself in it. She began to dry her hair and edged cautiously into the bedroom.

Among the remains of the chair were the remains of the Professor. She realized it would be impolite, not to say cold-hearted, to leave them there and Hazel winced as she thought of yet another potential confrontation with Mrs Day if that pain in the neck should discover her latest catastrophe.

A small brush and pan from the bathroom proved to be the only means of cleaning up the ashes so with trepidation and a feeling of nausea, Hazel began to sweep of the ashes. She was wondering what exactly she should do with them – dispensing them via the toilet did occur to her but she resisted that temptation as profane – when in the middle of the ashes, she saw a small clear plastic bag. She brushed ash away from it to get a clearer look. The bag contained a medium sized key and a much smaller one. Hazel was just reaching for it when she froze. From the passageway came the sound of approaching footsteps.

An instinct made Hazel kick the plastic bag under the wardrobe out of sight.

She stood erect and drew the robe tightly around her as she waited.

A shadow passed over the door and she saw the intruder.

It was Tommy.

Belinda received no answer when she knocked on Hazel's hotel door the next morning. Thinking that her friend was possibly in the shower and didn't hear, she went to meet Mark in the reception lounge where he was waiting before returning home to work. Belinda asked the girl at the reception desk to ring Hazel's room but there was no answer. So assuming that Hazel had already left for the Manor House or was in a mood and simply not answering, a not uncommon occurrence with Hazel, Belinda joined Mark in the lounge. He was looking serious. He took her hand as she sat next to him.

"Before I go, I have to tell you something."

"Whatever's the matter? You look worried."

Mark looked at her.

"I've been waiting for the right time to tell you because I didn't know how you'd react, but there never seemed to be the right time, so here goes. You know I want us to marry and I know you've felt you weren't quite ready for that, so I have to tell you that things have changed."

Belinda's heart skipped a beat. Was there someone else?

"You know my father died recently," Mark continued, "and things are different now."

Belinda gave a small sigh of relief. It wasn't someone else.

"How different?" she said.

"Well the fact is my father was a Baronet, as you know, and it's an hereditary title of honour. Queen Victoria bestowed it on my Grandfather for his improvement on industrial machinery at the time."

"Mark, why are you telling me all this?" said Belinda.

"Because my father inherited the title and now that he's gone, the title comes to me."

Belinda gave a cry of delight. "But how wonderful. Will you be called Sir Mark?

Mark took hold of both her hands and looked into her eyes.

"Yes. And if we marry ... you will be Lady Sallinger."

Belinda stared at him for a moment and then burst out laughing. She couldn't stop. Mark tried to stop her but the more he tried, the more she laughed. Several hotel guests were amused by her behaviour and wondered what the joke was. Eventually she calmed down and choking back a final giggle said: "Mark, you can't be serious."

"I'm afraid I am. So you see, I wanted to make you aware of it and give you time to think what it would mean if we marry."

Belinda was silent as the true meaning of what Mark was telling her began to sink in.

"It's been bothering me for weeks," he said, "how to tell you, because I don't want it to make any difference to us. I was frightened that you'd think it stupid or ridiculous or that you'd want no part of it. Believe me, it won't make any difference to the way I feel about you. I'm sorry to have dropped it on you like this, but you had to know sometime." Mark looked at his watch. "I must be off if I'm to reach Bath in time for my meeting." He stood up and helped Belinda to her feet. "Think it over and we can talk about it further when I come back."

Belinda looked dazed.

"Cheer up," Mark said. "They don't chop our heads off in England, well, not in recent times anyway."

Belinda gave a weak smile as he embraced her and kissed her goodbye. After he left she sat down again still bewildered by what he had told her. She gave another giggle at the absurdity of it but then was serious as she realised that what he had said was the truth. How would she deal with it? Gathering her wits about her she went down to collect her hire car, Mark having taken his.

As she approached the road to take her to the house she saw St Martin's Church and, remembering that she had planned to visit it, and feeling that it might be a quiet place to contemplate what marriage to Mark would mean, she pulled over and stopped outside the Lynch Gate.

The path to the entrance of the small church ran slightly uphill past a myriad of headstones with the graveyard encompassing three sides of the building. A magpie, perched on the top of the tower, watched her approach with caution ready to take wing should she prove to be an enemy.

As Belinda entered the porch a neatly dressed middle-aged woman, who was placing fresh flowers in vases, looked up and greeted her with a warm smile. Belinda sensed she would have no time for contemplation.

"Hello, dear. Welcome to St Martin's. Have you been here before?"

"No," said Belinda, "I'm just working here in Canterbury at the moment and I've often passed by and always wanted to visit."

"You know it's the oldest Christian Church in England still in use?" said the woman with a pride that suggested she'd had something to do with its origins. "Queen Bertha worshipped here and in the year 597, here in this church, St Augustine baptized her husband Ethelbert, the King of Kent, and that made England a Christian country. Although I sometimes wonder about that these days."

Belinda wandered into the tiny church.

"You said you're working here. What work is that?" asked the woman, as she carried a full vase of flowers to the altar.

"Only for a short time. I'm working down at the Manor House."

The woman turned to look at Belinda.

"Oh, you're one of those down from London doing the valuation for Muriel Mowbray."

"Not from London," said Belinda, wondering if there was anyone in Canterbury who didn't know what she and Hazel were doing. "We came from Bath."

The woman looked dubious. "Maireid Sullivan told me London, but if you say Bath, well I suppose you know best, but Maireid is mostly always right – about everything."

"Well, you can tell Miss Sullivan that for once she has made a mistake.

"Yes. Yes, that's right. I can." The woman brightened and was already playing in her mind's eye the scene where she would bring Maireid Sullivan down a peg or two. They walked back down the aisle to the porch where the woman sorted out more flowers.

"You know Miss Mowbray then," said Belinda.

The woman gave a tiny shake of her head that indicated disapproval.

"Oh, everyone knows Muriel Mowbray." She stopped as though in thought. "You know, I haven't thought about her in years."

"Miss Mowbray?" said Belinda.

"Good Lord no. No, I mean the Professor's wife. Mrs de Gray. She was a wonderful woman. She always worshiped here."

"Yes, I'd heard that."

"She always made sure we had plenty of flowers and helped out whenever she could."

Picking up another vase of flowers she proceeded up the aisle to the altar with Belinda following.

"I believe she's buried here in the church yard," said Belinda.

"Yes, dear, up in the newer section, that's where you'll find her. Such a sweet soul. It was a tragedy when she was taken from us. A fall down the stairs. A broken neck." She looked dolefully at Belinda. "The day of the Lord will come like a thief in the night." She nodded her head sharply to verify that her statement was a true and profound theological fact, thereby delivering a silent challenge to Belinda to deny it.

"Now as for Muriel Mowbray, she's never set foot in here, not once in all the years she was with the Professor as his secretary. Well, that's what she called herself. There's many around here who would call it something else."

They returned to the flowers in the porch.

"So Miss Mowbray was with the Professor all the time he was married?" said Belinda.

The woman grimaced.

"All the time. Shameful." She abruptly put her hand to her forehead. "No wait, I tell a lie. There was a time she wasn't there. It was just after the Professor married. She went away and we all thought good riddance to bad rubbish, but she came back and stayed on."

"How long was she away? Can you remember?"

"A year or so. No, about a year. I remember thinking at the time that she couldn't even give the newlyweds a year to themselves."

"How did the Professor's wife take that?"

"Like the saint she was," said the woman. "She trusted the Professor, although why any woman would trust a man is beyond me, but she did and then she had that awful fall and was taken from us."

The woman shook herself and resumed arranging the flowers.

"Well, I can't stand here gossiping. I must finish the preparations for the Taizé ceremony tonight."

"Taizé?"

"Yes, you should come. The church is lit by candles and we sing short chants of just a few words that express a central faith. We sing the words over and over and they gradually make a way into your soul."

"Thanks, I'll think about it," said Belinda. "I'd like to visit Mrs de Gray's grave while I'm here".

"It's just up the back there." The woman pulled a few January Gold daffodils from the bunch and handed them to Belinda. "Place them on the grave. She'll like them. Pleased to have met you and I hope that you will come and worship here during your stay. I should think you'll need all the blessings you can get if you have anything to do with the Manor House."

Belinda walked around beside the church and up the slight incline of the graveyard to an area of relatively modern graves. Most were in a state of neglect. She found the simple headstone bearing nothing more that the inscription 'Helen de Gray' and the date of her death. Nothing else to enlighten the mourner with regard to the woman's life. Belinda placed the flowers on the grave. Looking out over the tombs she could see the Bell Harry Tower of Canterbury Cathedral.

As she drove on, Belinda wondered about the woman's comment, 'you'll need all the blessings you can get'. Moreover she still found Mark's news spinning around in her brain. She decided, like Scarlet O'Hara, to think about that little bombshell tomorrow. But she would refrain from telling Hazel whose reaction she feared would be unsympathetic and barbed.

She drove up to the front door of the Manor House. Hazel's car was parked there, which did surprise Belinda, as Hazel wasn't given to early morning starts and it was only nine o'clock. As she passed the car she was further surprised to see the keys still in the ignition. Hazel was a stickler for security and was in constant fear of her Mercedes being stolen, so this was out of character. Belinda let herself into the house and anxiously called Hazel's name. Silence. A hurried check of the building revealed nothing. Hazel was not there.

Belinda, her brow furrowed with concern, dialled Hazel's phone, but was asked by a metallic voice to 'kindly leave a message'.

"Where are you? Ring me as soon as you get this," was the concerned message Belinda left. She went out to the Mercedes to see if it held any clues to Hazel's absence and opened the driver's door. Hazel's phone sat mutely on the passenger seat. She wandered back into the parlour trying to deduce what had happened and what she could do about it. It was useless ringing Mark. He was too far away to help. Should she ring the police? Well, maybe later, if Hazel didn't show up. She didn't want to be a fool if Hazel *did* show up smiling after one of her bawdy adventures.

And Hazel did show up. And smiling. The sound of a car as it roared to a skidding halt outside the house startled Belinda. She hurried to the window in time to see Hazel emerge from a bright red sports car. An expensive sports car. While this alone was enough to surprise Belinda, the fact that Hazel was dressed in a tight pair of men's jeans, a garish pair of trainers and a heavy fisherman's pullover, all topped off by a baseball cap favouring the New York Yankees, was something that Belinda had never thought to see and even now with the evidence before her very eyes, she doubted its validity. Mutton dressed as Ragout D'agneau.

Belinda could not see the driver but Hazel waved goodbye to whoever it was before entering the house. The sports car took off at an enormous rate, tyres squealing as it circled the fountain, then sped away with enough noise to wake the dead.

The two women confronted each other in the entrance hall.

"Where have you been?" said Belinda hotly. She was still in shock at seeing Hazel dressed as she was.

"I spent the night with a friend," said Hazel, annoyed at Belinda's censorious attitude. She walked into the parlour. "If it's any of your business."

Belinda followed her.

"No it's not usually, but I was concerned when you were missing and your car was left here with the keys in it."

"Oh, I forgot those."

"And you've been smoking. You reek of smoke. Who was it this time?" said Belinda. "Anyone we know?"

"Yes. Tommy," said Hazel with a gloating smile.

Belinda stared at her.

"But only the other day you suspected him of being a murderer."

"That's why I went with him, to see what I could find out."

Belinda rolled her eyes.

"Oh, please. Don't expect me to fall for that. We both know why you went with him."

Hazel looked her up and down.

"And who are you pray? My mother? OK, I admit I went with him because I wanted it to be fun. And it was. And yes, we were both careful." She gave a girlish giggle, which Belinda thought rather disturbing. "He smuggled me into his room at the University, I felt like a teenager. It was such fun." She smiled at the thought. "Believe me, Belinda, when you get to my age, you too will want a bit of fun, a chance to feel young again and to do something stupid."

"And where did Tommy get such an expensive sports car from?" said Belinda.

"He stole it," Hazel said with a note of admiration in her voice. "And don't give me that look, Miss Goody Two shoes," she continued when she saw the disapproving expression on Belinda's face. "And you needn't remind me he's half my age."

"More than half," said Belinda.

Hazel took a step closer, a dangerous glint in her eye.

"You're hardly in a position to criticize my behaviour. You dangle Mark on a string. 'Will I? won't I'? when he wants to marry you, while you have your boyfriend, Brad, lusting after you all the way from Australia. Those without sin, sweetheart, those without sin." She folded her arms defying Belinda to deny she was right.

Belinda sighed. If only Hazel knew how much more complicated her relationship with Mark had become. But what she said was true.

"I'm sorry, I'm a bit out of sorts; it's just that I was worried. Of course you can do what you want." There was a short silence. "But a stolen car, Hazel. You could have been arrested."

"Well, I wasn't," said Hazel with an air that implied she was unimpeachable. "And anyway he's returning the car today. They probably haven't missed it."

"Why are you wearing his clothes?"

"Because I didn't have any on," said Hazel, as though it was perfectly natural for her to be in a state of undress when she met a man.

Belinda wasn't sure she wanted to know why Hazel was naked and required men's attire.

"But where did you meet him?"

"That's what I wanted to tell you," said Hazel excitedly. "I came back here last night to search Miss Mowbray's room to see if I could find anything." Her previous attempt which had resulted in Mrs Day finding her hanging from the wardrobe, Hazel had kept to herself. "Tommy turned up. It seems he was planning to do some searching himself. Remember he has a key and he's obviously keen to find the missing USB computer file. That's the reason – well part of the reason – I went with him. I was hoping I'd be able to find out what he knows."

"And did you?" said Belinda.

"Need you ask," said Hazel with a smirk.

"I'm talking about the missing file," snapped Belinda.

"Yes, I'm sorry," said Hazel, not meaning a word of it. "But seriously, I did find something myself. Just before Tommy arrived I found …"

She froze as she saw Mrs Day standing at the doorway. "I'll tell you later," she whispered. Not wishing to confront Mrs Day, Hazel brushed past the woman and went out to her car. Belinda and Mrs Day watched her climb into it and drive away, dressed as a teenager – and a teenaged boy at that.

"Has that woman ever considered the idea of consulting a doctor?" said Mrs Day archly.

Belinda resumed work. Later in the day she had strolled down to the near-derelict stables to see if there was anything that could be salvaged. She knew Miss Mowbray didn't consider there to be anything of value remaining, but Belinda felt it worth checking: one never knew what surprises it may hold. She was rewarded for her instinct as there was a magnificent Landau carriage covered in dirt and cobwebs but easily restorable and worth quite a lot of money. A small Fly was also salvageable. Pleased with her discovery, Belinda sat on a pile of boxes to make notes about her discovery and was about to return to the house when a movement in the orchard caught her eye. She glimpsed a dark shape moving through the stunted trees. It was the black top hat worn by the figure that caused her to spring up. Looking around the door she saw clearly that it was the man she'd witnessed leaving the funeral parlour and therefore was Peter Jones. He moved towards the rear of the house. Gingerly, Belinda stepped down into the orchard and, keeping her distance, followed him. Peter disappeared around the back of the building.

Belinda moved cautiously along the side of the house and peered around the corner. Peter was standing at the kitchen door talking to his mother, Mrs Jones, who stood in the doorway wiping her hands on her apron. Under the cover of some shrubs Belinda edged closer to hear what they were saying. Peter seemed excited and his mother appeared to be trying to calm him down. Belinda could only hear the odd word and edged closer.

"I've told you not to worry, son," said Mrs Jones soothingly.

"But what has happened to Umm Walad?" said Peter in a distressed voice.

"I've told you before, Peter. Forget about Umm Walad. Everything will be all right. Now, you go off home and rest."

"But I want to go to the Cathedral Archives. They may have something for me to do."

"Well, do that if you must, but don't overexcite yourself, and make sure you're home in time for tea."

Peter bent down and kissed his mother's cheek.

Realising he was leaving and not wishing to be caught eavesdropping, Belinda turned and hurried back to the parlour. She waited at the door until Peter came in view. He wore his usual costume of black coat, scarf and hat and lanky hair hung down to his collar. His face was long and drawn and his skin colourless. Only his dark eyes seemed alive.

"Hello," she called, "are you Peter?"

Peter stopped in surprise and stood silently appraising Belinda. She approached slowly. His eyes alert and mistrustful watched as she drew near.

"I'm Belinda Lawrence. I'm working for Miss Mowbray."

Peter dug his hands into his frock coat pockets, glanced at the house and back to Belinda. She gave him a smile.

"I know you worked with Professor de Gray on his book." Peter nodded slowly. "That must have been a great experience," continued Belinda, hoping she was gaining the man's confidence. "Do you know what it was about?"

Peter grinned knowingly. "Yes, St Thomas. I helped with the research."

"So you'd know a lot about Thomas Becket?"

"More than most people," said Peter with a hint of pride in his voice.

"Then you must know what it was that Professor de Gray was so excited about."

Peter dropped his gaze and remained silent.

Realizing that she'd get nothing more from him at this point, Belinda changed tack.

"And I understand that you spend time at the Cathedral Archives."

This seemed to stir Peter into a response. He visibly relaxed and his eyes lit up with pleasure.

"Yes. I'm going to work there, or at least I hope that I can. All I need is …" His voice trailed off and he stood staring at Belinda.

"Qualifications?" said Belinda.

Peter frowned.

"Or if I could find something the Archives wanted, perhaps they would take me," he said with childish enthusiasm. "Do you think they would?"

"Oh, I'm sure they would," said Belinda, hoping she sounded convincing. "The Archives must be a very exciting place to work. I'd love to see what they've collected."

Peter gave a crooked smile.

"I'm going to the Archives now," he said smugly.

"Are you? Do you think I could come with you?"

Peter looked dubious. "I'm not sure."

"I've got a car, I could drive you there and you could ask them," said Belinda.

It's a bit like persuading a child with a toffee, she thought.

Peter considered the offer and decided he would accept.

"Yes. All right, and on the way I can tell you about the crown." Again his eyes lit up with pleasure.

Crown? What crown? Belinda was momentarily puzzled but assumed that Peter would explain on the journey.

He didn't but he kept up an excited chatter about St Thomas all the way into Canterbury and seemed eager to impress with his knowledge. So much so that instead of visiting the Archives,

Belinda found herself being led by Peter into the Cathedral. They stopped at Trinity Chapel where the shrine of St Thomas had been displayed before it was destroyed by Henry VIII.

"This is where St Thomas's tomb stood," said Peter.

"Yes, I know," said Belinda.

But Peter was in full flight and would not be stopped. Holding his top hat by the brim and turning it round and round nervously, his enthusiasm transformed him as he prattled on. "It was covered with plates of pure gold but you could hardly see the gold because of hundreds of precious stones, diamonds, rubies, sapphires, emeralds. The King of France sent a ruby the size of a thumbnail, they say. Some years ago pieces of rose-coloured marble where found in the river, the same marble as here." He pointed to the floor.

"And so they might have come from the tomb when it was destroyed," said Belinda

They stepped away from Trinity Chapel.

"Did you know there are two secret chambers in the Cathedral," said Peter in a confidential voice, rather like a child with a riddle.

"No," said Belinda with a grin, "but you know about them, don't you?"

Peter gave a self-satisfied smile.

"They're perfect for hiding away treasures or …"

"Or relics?"

Peter glanced at her sharply but ignored her question.

"In St Andrew's Chapel, there's one about six feet off the ground and you need a ladder to get up to it. There's another in the Chapel of St Gabriel."

"Where's that?' said Belinda.

"In the crypt."

Belinda gave a tiny shudder.

"I'll give that a miss. I don't have happy memories of the crypt."

But Peter was engrossed in his chatter and enjoying showing off his knowledge to a new audience.

"The entrance is through a hole that's hidden by an altar. There's no window and the roof is covered with strange twelfth century paintings."

Before Belinda could say anything more he took her arm and propelled her further on to the far east end of the Cathedral and the small circular chapel there. He stood gazing at it in awe. Belinda waited for an explanation.

"What's this?"

When Peter spoke his voice had dropped to a reverential hush. "This is the Corona. Becket's Crown."

Belinda looked into the rounded chapel. There was a small plain altar, lit in a myriad of colours by the light from the magnificent stained glass windows.

"Why is it called that?"

"Some years after Thomas was murdered," said Peter, in a rather touching academic fashion, "this end of the Cathedral was destroyed by fire. During the reconstruction, the Corona Tower was built here to hold a relic which was the crown of St Thomas's head, which was cut off when the knights, Hugh de Moreville and William de Tracy struck him with their swords."

"So the rest of his remains were in the shrine?"

Peter nodded.

"Why separate them?" said Belinda. "It seems an odd thing to do."

"In medieval times the head of a saint was regarded as the most holy and important relic, and in Thomas's case, the crown of his head was separated from his body in an act of murder. Therefore it was regarded as the holiest relic, over and above the rest of his body."

"What happened to it? Was it destroyed at the same time as the shrine?"

Peter turned and they began to make their way back through the Cathedral past the tomb of the Black Prince.

"No one knows what happened to it. It was probably destroyed. But some argue that it didn't exist in the first place. Others that it contained the whole of Thomas's skull, but there's evidence that his damaged skull was with the rest of his bones in the shrine."

"Like the bones that were dug up in the crypt?" said Belinda.

Peter stopped and looked at her.

"You know about them?"

"Yes," said Belinda, moving on. Peter caught up with her. "And I seem to remember that part of that skull was missing. So it's possible that the Professor discovered something about the bones." She turned to face Peter. "Did he?"

Peter looked evasive and fiddled with his hat. He glanced at his watch.

"I must go. I'm expected home for tea."

He turned and sprinted down the nave, brushing through a group of tourists. Belinda followed slowly, watching as he ran out the door. She was certain now he knew what the Professor had discovered.

Chapter Eight

When Belinda returned to the hotel that evening it was to find Hazel ensconced in the lounge, halfway through a gin and tonic and thankfully dressed in her own clothes. Belinda plonked herself down on the sofa, kicked off her shoes and related her experience with Peter and his mother and later their visit to the Cathedral. Hazel peered at her over the top of her glass as she listened, a mischievous smile lingering on her lips as though she had a secret, as indeed she had.

Belinda yawned and rubbed her weary eyes.

"Do you think it's worth continuing with the inventory?"

"May as well," said Hazel. "We're just about through, and besides if we leave now we'll never know who murdered the Professor."

"True, but do you think we ever will? And what if Mrs Day was wrong about the blood? Maybe it was just a heart attack and he hit his head on the desk as they said."

"You give up too easily." Hazel put her empty glass on the table. "Besides I can assure you there has been dirty doings going on."

"I thought you'd cornered the market on dirty doings," said Belinda repressing another yawn.

"I'll ignore that," said Hazel, leaning forward in her chair. "I've got evidence."

Belinda was suddenly wide awake. "What sort of evidence?"

Hazel lowered her voice to a dramatic whisper. "Two things. Firstly I spoke with the Professor's lawyer and there is a possibility that Miss Mowbray forged his signature on a letter requesting he be buried immediately after death. Secondly, remember I said I'd tell you something later? Well, last night, before Tommy arrived I found the Professor's ashes."

Belinda's eyes widened, but before she could utter a word, Hazel continued: "They were in Miss Mowbray's room on top of the wardrobe." Here she paused. Should she tell Belinda about her fall and the resulting mess and how she and Tommy had spent an hilarious half-hour cleaning up the chaos? She decided against it. "Hidden in the ashes was a package. What do you think was in it? Keys."

"Keys?"

"Two keys. One large, one small."

"Where are they?" Belinda's interest was now well aroused.

"Under the wardrobe."

"Under the wardrobe?" said Belinda.

"Stop repeating everything I say," said Hazel impatiently. "I had to hide them under there when I heard someone coming. It turned out to be Tommy, and as you know I was then otherwise engaged, so I have to get back into the room to get the keys."

"Well, we can do that tomorrow."

"Not as easy at it sounds. For reasons best left unsaid, I can't afford for Mrs Day to find me in there again. So we'll have to wait until she's gone for the day."

Belinda was dying to ask why Hazel was anxious to avoid Mrs Day. And what did she mean 'again'? Belinda thought it better not to ask for an explanation just then. Time would reveal all, she felt certain.

"Now," said Hazel, "what sort of person hides something in a person's ashes? Whatever those keys are for, it's bleedin' obvious they're important to Miss Mowbray and for some reason she doesn't want anyone to find them."

"Hiding them in the ashes does seem a fairly safe place," said Belinda. "Who'd ever think of looking there? Or even want to? So you were searching Miss Mowbray's room? Did you find anything else of interest?"

"No, only that the woman has no taste in clothes. Nothing else, other than a drawer full of old diaries. There must be forty years or more of them."

"Really? Interesting?"

"Not from what I could see. Full of details about her boring work."

Belinda looked thoughtful.

"How long ago was it the Professor got married, do you remember?"

Hazel scratched her neck.

"Let's see. I think you said Mrs Day told you thirty years or so. Why?"

Belinda shook her head. "Nothing. It was just a thought."

But she seemed distracted by that thought for the rest of the evening.

The next day was taken up with their usual activities but Belinda and Hazel both kept an eye on the clock awaiting the time that Mrs Day would put on her bumblebee coat, mount her bicycle and ride off into the murky sunset. Hazel's discovery of Miss Mowbray's diaries had sparked an interest in Belinda so that when eventually Mrs Day called in to say goodbye, her curiosity about the books overshadowed Hazel's discovery of the keys.

The two women watched Mrs Day cycle off before hurrying down the passage way to Miss Mowbray's room. As they entered, Hazel headed for the wardrobe but was stopped by Belinda.

"Where did you find the diaries?"

"What do you want them for?"

Belinda shrugged.

"I'm not sure. It's just an idea I have."

Hazel walked over to the dresser and opened the bottom drawers.

"They're here, but you'll get no joy from them, I can assure you."

Belinda reached down and drew some of the diaries out. They were small and appeared to be in order of years. She began to sort through them as Hazel watched bemused by this development.

"What are you looking for?"

"I'm looking for those dated about thirty years ago," said Belinda as she continued to search.

"Well, you can waste your time; I'm interested in the keys," said Hazel. She went to the wardrobe and got down on her hands and knees to peer underneath. It was dark and she could see nothing. She stretched her hand into the shadowy recess. The adhesive chill of a cobweb brushed her hand and a black spider ran up her arm. Her shriek caused Belinda to drop the diaries in fright. Hazel, with a shiver of apprehension, once more slid her arm under the wardrobe, this time more cautiously.

Belinda bent to pick up the diaries and discovered they were the years she was looking for. She took a quick glance through them but realised that she would need to sit down and spend time searching from first to last in detail if she was to find what she was looking for. If indeed she knew what that was. She began to replace the other diaries in the drawers.

Hazel, by stretching her arm to its full extent, was barely able to reach the plastic bag and had just caught it in her fingertips when the sound of approaching footsteps was heard.

The two women looked at each other.

Mrs Day?

With an agility that surprised her, Hazel made a dive and slid under the bed. Belinda, faced with no such easy option, glanced about for a place to hide. The bathroom was an obvious choice but there was a danger that Mrs Day would go in there. There was only one answer so she stepped into the wardrobe, burying herself in Miss Mowbray's dresses.

From under the bed Hazel had a limited view of the doorway. Beneath the fringe of the bedcover she watched two legs enter from the passageway and pause at the door. The owner of the legs was wearing trousers and men's boots. Clearly not Mrs Day, unless she had a secret vice and was given to cross-dressing.

The legs proceeded to the dresser and a hand reached down and opened the bottom drawers. Hazel squiggled about to see who it was. It was a man she didn't know.

Belinda peered through the slit in the wardrobe door and watched in amazement as Peter Jones opened a carrier bag and began to place the diaries in it.

"What do you think you're doing?" came a raucous challenge from the bed.

Peter dropped the bag in fright and looked at the bed.

"They don't belong to you," said the wardrobe.

If Peter had ever doubted his sanity, here was proof. The furniture was talking to him. The surreal experience continued for him when the door of the wardrobe opened and Belinda stepped down into the room, a polyester crepe dress sliding off her shoulder, while from under the bed Hazel emerged, covered in fluff balls.

"Do you know whose diaries they are?" said Belinda.

Peter recognised Belinda but was unsure of the older woman now picking fluff out of her hair. With his pulse slowly returning to normal, he nodded. "Yes. They're Umm Walad's." As he uttered the words Peter gave a panicky, guilty look. "Whose?" the two women chorused.

Peter was silent.

Belinda slipped the four diaries she held, behind her and hoped that Peter hadn't seen them.

"Hazel, you haven't met Peter. This is Mrs Jones' son."

Peter and Hazel exchanged glances. Neither was impressed.

"They're Miss Mowbray's diaries, Peter. Why are you taking them?"

Peter shuffled his feet.

"My mother told me to collect them."

"Why would she do that?" demanded Hazel sternly.

Peter looked at her with trepidation. He didn't like this woman.

"Because Miss Mowbray's in hospital and my mother thought someone might go through them and read her private thoughts. We're going to hold them safe until she comes home."

Belinda gave Hazel a knowing look.

"I think that's probably a good idea. Go ahead, Peter. Take them all."

Relieved that he now had the chance to escape from these two women, Peter hurriedly filled the carrier bag with the remaining diaries. As he dropped the last one in he stood up and looked at Belinda as though awaiting permission to leave.

"Good evening, Peter. Give my regards to your mother."

Peter put on his top hat and with the bag firmly in his grasp fled from the room. They heard his footsteps as he ran down the passageway and out the door into the approaching night.

The two keys lay on the parlour desk. One was an old iron key that looked as though it was made for a door, the other a smaller ornate key similar to one used to lock a jewel box. Belinda picked up the larger one and inspected it. Hazel hurried in, drying her hands on a towel. The plastic bag had some of the ashes clinging to it so she'd disposed of it and spent a little time scrubbing her hands lest some of the cadaverous dust should remain on her.

"What do you make of them?"

"This one has something written on it," said Belinda as she turned the key around. It was a plain barrel key about five inches long with a circular bow and it was there that some worn lettering appeared. "I can just make it out 'd' 'e'."

"De Grey," said Hazel. "Am I right?"

"Yes. It's de Grey. It looks very old."

Hazel took it from Belinda and examined it.

"At least seventeenth century, I'd say. Could be older." She put it back on the desk. "What about the other one?"

Belinda picked it up. It was gold in colour and about an inch in length. The bow was an ornate design.

"It's very pretty."

"About eighteenth century at a guess, but probably late in the century," said Hazel, taking the key from Belinda.

"So. What do you think they're for?"

Hazel dropped the small key onto the desk. "It's obvious they're connected with the USB file. My guess is that Miss Mowbray has hidden it somewhere in the house and these keys will lead us to it."

Belinda gave a scornful laugh. "You mean search the entire house? Do you have any idea of how many rooms and objects there are that require a key to open them? We'll be here all year."

"Not necessarily. All items have been catalogued in my inventory and those that require a key will be easy to locate. That'll make it easier."

Belinda gave a sigh and stood up.

"Well, it can wait until tomorrow. It's late and I'm hungry." She put on her coat and picked up the diaries that she'd taken. Hazel closed her laptop and gathered her things. They switched off the light, locked the front door and walked to their cars.

"Your friend Peter is a strange one," said Hazel.

"Strange, to say the least," agreed Belinda.

"What was it he said about whose diaries they were? Oh Wally?" Belinda smiled.

"That's not it but something like it." She stopped as she opened her car door. "That's funny, I heard him use it earlier when he was talking to his mother. 'Um' something. He said 'what's happened to 'Um something'. I thought it might have been a missing cat."

"Cats don't write diaries," said Hazel, as she placed the laptop in her car, "and I don't buy that story about his mother taking the diaries to prevent anyone reading the old biddy's personal thoughts. Believe me, from what I saw she's never had a thought, personal or otherwise."

This observation proved to be more or less true as Belinda discovered later that night as she settled into her bed and opened the first year of the diaries. Apart from Miss Mowbray's name and the year concerned, the front pages revealed little, as did most of the other pages. They were, as Hazel had indicated, mostly related to her work for the Professor. Occasionally there was a reference to extreme weather conditions or her mild ill health or repairs to the house that she and the Professor were renting in Canterbury at the time. Once she reported that the Professor had suffered gout and on another occasion he'd been on an extended trip to London.

Some weeks after that entry, another detailed the visit to Canterbury of a Miss Helen de Goderigge.

"This is more like it," Belinda muttered.

There were no further entries until a month later Belinda read, 'the London Cow back again'. Thereafter there were more entries that had the initials 'LC' at the top of the page, which indicated to Belinda that the London Cow, that being Helen de Goderigge, had visited the Professor regularly. This changed over the weeks to 'Walter to LC' and this entry was repeated and increased as the months past.

Finally Belinda came to an entry that read, 'Walter revealed to me today that he is to marry the LC. They are to live in the Manor House she inherited. I hate her. He cares for the house more than her I'm certain. I don't know what to say to him now. He doesn't listen to me. I shall have to go away. There is no other way and I will have to deal with it myself.'

The remaining pages for that year were blank. Belinda picked up the next year's diary. It hardly seemed worth the while for Miss Mowbray to have bothered keeping a diary because the few entries that were in it were scattered over the twelve months, with a reference to an address in Cheshire and later another in York and finally one in Holland Road, Kensington. Other entries were little more than covert hieroglyphics such as 'dr2', 'bookh', 'Today?' and 'My Rock'.

It wasn't until near the end of the diary that Belinda found any entries of value.

'Today I wrote to Walter.'

'Walter replied today. I am to meet him at Kensington tube station at noon.' This was followed by a further entry.

'We spent the day at Richmond. Walter has asked me to return to him. I will go. My Rock is mine.' Tucked in between the pages was an old underground rail ticket.

There were no further entries. The next two diaries again recorded the largely dry academic work that Miss Mowbray undertook for the Professor. There were only two notes of a personal nature in the last book.

'The LC died today'. Three weeks later another entry, 'My Rock left me today. I am heartbroken.'

Belinda put the diary down. Again Miss Mowbray had made mention of 'Rock' but its meaning was no clearer. She knew she wouldn't sleep that night as she thought over the meanings of the cryptic diary entries. Not to mention Mark's news and the prospect of being Lady Sallinger.

The next morning Belinda found Hazel at the computer making notes of the various items in the house that required a key. She read out to her the entries in Miss Mowbray's diaries.

"Rock?" said Hazel. "What does she mean, Rock? Did she fantasize about Rock Hudson?"

"I don't think Miss Mowbray ever fantasized about anything," said Belinda, "but it does confirm that she went away and then returned at the Professor's request, at least according to what she says."

"After he'd been married only a year."

"Well, officially she was returning to take up her old position as secretary."

"I wonder how his wife took that."

"We'll probably never know, but I'd still like to find out what all the other vague entries mean. She must have been up to something in the year she was away," said Belinda.

Hazel took her list of items, along with the small gold key, and they began the tedious task of attempting to fit the key into the countless locks contained in the bric-a-brac, curios and knick-knacks scattered about the house. By the time Mrs Jones brought them their lunch their wrists were aching from all the twisting and turning.

"Well, we've just about done the lot," said Belinda as she massaged her wrist. "If you do the remaining ones after lunch, I'll start on the doors."

The large iron key although it looked like a door key proved not to be so and Belinda had tried all the various doors without success. Mrs Day had given her curious glances as she went from room to room but seemed not over interested in her activity. Mrs Jones paused as she returned to the kitchen with the lunch tray and watched Belinda move from door to door, but when Belinda turned to look at her, the woman turned and left without comment.

Belinda arrived at the last door which was the storage room. Again she was disappointed. She stood in the doorway the key in her hand wondering what on earth it was for. The sight of the clutter in the room reminded her that she should search through it in case there was an item of value buried there. Some empty cardboard boxes and a few dusty watercolours looked worthless but a number of old prints were worth checking, one never knew, but they could wait until tomorrow. She was about to leave and report her disappointment to Hazel when she glimpsed the edge of a large chest almost hidden by old worn fabrics and rugs. With some effort Belinda managed to lift the dusty material and heavy carpets off the coffer. Sneezing from the dust she wiped her eyes. The exposed container was about five feet in length and four feet deep and proved to be a late 16th century Elizabethan oaken chest, the front of which had a central foliate geometric motif flanked by leaf-carved panels. It was framed with floral embellishments, by means of inlay, and although of great age it was in good condition.

Belinda dropped to her knees in front of it and ran her hand over the ancient surface. She tried to lift the lid but it wouldn't budge. There was a lock below the lid and on the spur of the moment, Belinda inserted the old iron key. To her surprise it fitted and the key turned. Holding her breath in excitement and wondering what was in the chest, Belinda lifted the lid.

Chapter Nine

A crisp white envelope almost glowed in stark contrast to the dark mouldy jumble beneath it. The chest was filled to overflowing with old fabrics, newspapers brown with age, torn magazines, assorted trinkets, an old teapot or two and several items of decaying clothing. Resting on top of this mountain of debris the envelope, its surface unsullied by time, was clearly a recent arrival.

Belinda reached down and picked up the envelope. She could feel the outline of a small hard object and even before she tore it open she knew it contained what they had been searching for. Excitedly she drew it out and examined it. It was indeed a computer USB, which she was certain, held the file containing the missing chapter to the Professor's book.

Cautiously she placed it in the pocket of her slacks, replaced the envelope and closed and locked the chest. Pocketing the key she went in search of Hazel. As she turned a corner in the passageway she almost ran into Mrs Jones. The woman excused herself and hurried away. Belinda wondered what she was doing in that part of the house, as she usually left after serving lunch and was rarely out of the kitchen. But she was far too excited to worry about that as she bounded up the stairs to Hazel who was working in the Great Hall. Hazel looked up at her entrance.

Belinda held the USB aloft as though it was the Holy Grail.

"Found it!" she cried.

Hazel gave a whoop and pushed back her chair. Together they hurried down the stairs to the parlour. Hazel switched on the Professor's computer and Belinda inserted the USB. Clicking on Start and then My Computer, Hazel clicked on Back Up. The computer screen went black and a message came up, 'USB Lock. Status. Protected.

Hazel hit the desk in frustration. "Bugger. It needs a password."

As if to confirm her belief, the screen mockingly changed to, 'Please enter your password'.

Belinda gave a sigh of disappointment. "Oh no, and we're so close. What do we do now?"

"We could try and guess whatever password was used, but that could take forever. But I'll try his name." Hazel typed in 'Walter de Gray'. They were rewarded with a new screen message.

'Warning: USB will self destruct after 5 more invalid password attempts'.

"That means we're stuffed," said Hazel dispiritedly. "Without the password we may as well not have the bloody thing."

She gave the desk a thump to show her grief.

"Try de Grey. With an 'e'. He had a different spelling."

Hazel dutifully typed this in, but up came the warning of only four more invalid password attempts.

"People often use the most obvious passwords," said Belinda. Try Thomas."

Once again the password was rejected leaving them with only three more chances to open the file.

"Perhaps the Professor gave the password to someone else," Belinda said, trying to rescue the situation.

"Like who?" said Hazel gruffly.

"Well, Miss Mowbray for a start, after all it was she who hid the file, so it seems obvious she would know how to open it."

"True," said Hazel, "but let's not forget the woman is in hospital with half her head missing and total memory loss."

Belinda sat down, her head in her hands. "Rats," she said with some force.

"I think it's time for a double gin," said Hazel as she rose.

"And I think I'll join you," muttered Belinda dolefully.

The tonic water fizzed in the gin as Belinda and Hazel eased themselves onto the sofas in the hotel lounge, disappointed. The clinks of ice and the clinks of glass as they toasted their discovery were almost ear-splitting given the silence in the room. But it was a Pyrrhic victory and both women knew it.

Hazel summoned up the confidence to say: "Of course, apart from Miss Mowbray, whom we believe has the password, it's possible that others may know it."

"Such as?" said Belinda, sipping her drink.

"Well, we can rule out Mrs Day. I hardly imagine she'd have any interest in the matter and Mrs Jones even less I should think. Clearly both the publishers don't have it, so that leaves Tommy and Peter."

"And both of them had helped the Professor while he was writing."

"Exactly. Which means that somehow or other we have to find out if either of them, or both for that matter, know the password and if so, get them to tell us."

"But to do that we'd have to let them know we have the missing file."

Hazel took a large gulp of gin. What Belinda said was spot on. But there had to be a way around the problem.

"Not necessarily," she said after some thought, "You seem to have some understanding of that fruit cake, Peter. On the other hand I have a certain affinity with Master Tommy. Between us we should be able to worm out of them anything they know about the files, including the password."

Belinda wasn't so sure but she agreed to go along with Hazel's idea, after all 'nothing ventured, nothing gained'. But first, Belinda announced that she would travel to London the next morning to visit Miss Mowbray in hospital on the off chance that she was getting better and had recovered her memory.

As she left Victoria station and approached the hospital Belinda was startled to see Tommy as he came down the steps. She hardly recognised him as he had abandoned his usual 'I'm a University student and I'm the centre of the universe' look and was wearing an expensive tweed overcoat with a thick woollen scarf twisted around his neck and smart herringbone flat cap. He looked highly respectable, a man about town, and Belinda wondered what had brought about this transformation. It seemed clear to her he had been visiting Miss Mowbray and this alone was a mystery for although he obviously knew the woman, there had been no suggestion that they were friendly or that there was any reason why he would be concerned about her.

Tommy had crossed the street in the direction of Buckingham Palace Road and Belinda believed that he had not seen her as she'd drawn near; otherwise he would have made some vulgar suggestion of a sexual nature she felt sure. Instinctively she followed him, curious to see where he would lead her. She had to hurry to keep him in sight as he was striding along. Once he glanced back over his shoulder and Belinda ducked for cover into the entrance to the Royal Mews. She didn't want to have a confrontation with him and ventured out only when she saw he was continuing.

They passed in front of Buckingham Palace and Belinda lost sight of him as she got wedged within a group of excited American tourists, their cameras digitally recording every single moment of their tour to be used to cudgel into a somnambulistic state, their less adventurous neighbours upon their return. She eventually caught sight of him crossing the road and heading for Green Park, so with deft use of her elbows and with total disregard for bruised ribs and injured international feelings, was able to break free and keep him in sight until eventually she caught up and was close behind.

Once again Tommy turned to look back and Belinda dived behind a tree, feeling slightly stupid as though she was in a bad spy film and wondered what passers-by thought of her. They certainly gave her odd looks.

When she looked again, Tommy was still walking away. Feeling sure he hadn't seen her she resumed following him. As she reached Piccadilly she saw he had crossed the road and was waiting at the Green Park tube station bus stop. She lingered behind some people waiting for buses hoping that he would not look across the road and see her but his attention seemed to be directed to looking for the next bus.

As a bus eventually pulled up at his stop and screened her from his view, she took her life in her hands and quickly crossed the road. Fortunately the traffic was light but her action did cause a taxi driver a moment of consternation and he put his head out the taxi window to loudly give her some heartfelt advice and made a suggestion that she would win a prize for stupidity at Crufts Dog Show.

She boarded the bus hoping that Tommy wasn't sitting nearby but he was not to be seen and had obviously gone upstairs so Belinda took a seat towards the rear of the bus where she would have a view of the staircase. Someone had left a copy of the Daily Telegraph so she opened the paper and used it as a screen in case Tommy saw her when he descended the stairs.

As they approached the stop at Piccadilly Circus, Tommy descended the stairs. Belinda peered over the top of the newspaper. The bus stopped and he was first off with Belinda hurrying behind. Tommy made his way through the crowds down into Haymarket. Belinda followed at a safe distance. She wondered what he was up to and where he would lead her. He ducked into a Pizza Café.

Not wishing to be seen and wondering how long he would be in the café, she entered a coffee shop opposite and ordered a latte. She took it to a seat at the window where she could keep an eye on the Pizza shop. She'd barely taken her first sip when she saw Tommy emerge, pause, look around him, and then walk up Panton Street towards Leicester Square. Leaving her coffee she hurriedly crossed the road and followed.

As she approached the Square her foot caught on an uneven surface and the heel snapped off her shoe. With a curse she hurriedly picked up the shoe and heel and hobbled on. When she reached the Square she could see no sign of Tommy. He seemed to have disappeared. He could have gone into any of the buildings around the Square and not knowing how long he would be it seemed pointless to wait but she shuffled over and stood by the fountain and statue of Shakespeare. On inspecting her shoe she saw it was beyond immediate repair and rather than limp through London, she removed her good shoe and stuffed them in her shoulder bag.

Five minutes passed and Belinda began to think she was wasting her time. Her stockinged feet were frozen and hopping back and forth from one to the other did nothing to warm them and gave passers-by the impression she was a busker performing some lamentable rumba they considered not worth rewarding financially.

Disappointed, she was about to give up when Tommy emerged from a cinema doorway and hurried through to Charing Cross Road. Following in his footsteps, Belinda raced across the Square. She arrived in time to see him enter Cecil Court.

Crossing the road she peered around the corner of the narrow street. Tommy was standing looking in a shop window but talking to another man, who turned and hurried past Belinda, glancing at her stockinged feet as he did so and, presuming this to be a new fashion dictate, shook his head and went on his way wondering at the eccentricities of female fashions. She waited while Tommy continued browsing at other shop windows until he eventually walked into St Martin's Lane.

Belinda followed and to her great surprise he entered the building containing the publishing offices of Sir Justin Oliver. Her mind racing, she sought to make a connection between Tommy and the publisher. She approached the doorway and was startled when Tommy suddenly leapt out and threw his arms around her.

"I knew you couldn't stay away from me," he said giving a victorious smile. "You've been following me all the way from Victoria."

He may have changed his wardrobe but he hadn't changed his machismo manner, thought Belinda.

She broke free from his embrace.

"You idiot. Let go."

"I saw you arrive as I was leaving the hospital and saw you were following me, so I thought I'd lead you a merry dance, and I did," he chortled. "It's fun being the one who's stalked rather than being the stalker. Makes a nice change."

"You mean when you stalked us on New Year's Day at Greyfriars?" Belinda slapped at his hands as he tried to embrace her again.

"That was only a bit of fun. 007 stuff," Tommy sniggered. "If only you'd seen your face in Leicester Square when you thought you'd lost me. And I enjoyed the exhibition dance you gave."

Belinda was angry at being made a fool of.

"Why did you visit Miss Mowbray? And don't deny you did."

Tommy just laughed and looked at his watch.

"That's for me to know and you to find out. Now, I'm late for an appointment, so give us a kiss."

He leant forward to kiss her, but Belinda pushed him away. Ignoring her rejection and with another delighted laugh he bounded up the steps two at a time and disappeared behind the glass doors.

Belinda retraced her steps to the hospital via a shoe repair kiosk. The fact that Tommy had led her to Sir Justin's office probably indicated that he didn't know that she knew of its location within that building and therefore be able to make any connection between him and the publisher. Unless he didn't care if she knew or not, and judging by his usual audacious behaviour this could be the case. Assuming Tommy knew the password to open the missing file, he was in a position to do a deal with Sir Justin. Did he also know where the file had been hidden? And was his stalking only fun or something more ominous? She felt Tommy was capable of creating more exciting 'fun' on New Year's Day than following her. Had he been spying on them all the time they'd been in Canterbury, and was he doing it alone or under orders from someone else?

Her shoes repaired and her feet, though damp, tucked warmly

into their welcome protection Belinda, on arriving at the hospital, found Miss Mowbray had improved although the nurse advised she was still seriously ill. She was talking a little and her memory had partly returned but she was still confused.

"She rambles on," said the nurse. "You mustn't be fussed with some of the things she says, if she talks at all."

"Like what?" said Belinda.

"Oh the usual thing patients come out with if they think they're going to die. Confessions, asking for family members who are dead and buried, that sort of thing. Sins committed, you name it, most of course just rambling."

Belinda was permitted to visit for a few minutes and as she sat by the sleeping woman she noted there was a fresh vase of flowers. Had Tommy brought them?

Suddenly her hand was grasped in a vice-like grip. She turned to see Miss Mowbray staring at her with piercing eyes. She muttered something softly, which Belinda didn't hear. She bent closer.

"Awful sins," whispered Miss Mowbray.

Belinda gave her hand a reassuring squeeze.

"Don't you worry Miss Mowbray. You've nothing to be sorry for."

"It was murder, you know," said Miss Mowbray, her voice gaining in intensity. "I covered it up. But I hated him."

She fell silent for a moment. Belinda leaned closer still.

"The Professor? How did you cover it up?" she whispered.

Miss Mowbray's eyes flickered losing their intensity.

"The doctor. Money. Had him burned. Money."

"And you have his ashes, don't you?" Miss Mowbray gave a feeble smile. "And you know the password too," continued Belinda encouragingly.

But Miss Mowbray just stared at her blankly.

"Who are you? Are you a doctor?"

The nurse put her head around the door.

"Time to go, I'm afraid."

Belinda nodded and rose.

"Here's my telephone number. Can you let me know her progress?"

The nurse slipped the note into her pocket. Belinda looked at the woman in the bed, who now appeared to be sleeping again. She gathered her handbag and turned to leave. Miss Mowbray gave a low sigh.

"Samoht," she muttered.

Chapter Ten

"Thomas. It's Thomas spelled backwards. How simple. Why didn't I think of that?" Hazel switched on the computer.

Belinda had hurried back to Canterbury and to the Manor House. She relayed her brief visit to the hospital and what she understood to be a confession by Miss Mowbray admitting she'd killed the Professor. But her most gripping news was she believed the word Miss Mowbray had uttered, 'Samoht' was the secret password to open the missing file.

Holding her breath Hazel typed in the word S-A-M-O-H-T. There was a moment of suspense and up came the words,

'Warning: USB will self destruct after 2 more invalid password attempts'.

Both women stared at the screen in frustration.

"But I was sure that was it," cried Belinda. "What else would the word mean?"

"Sometimes passwords require numerals as well as words," said Hazel.

"But how can we guess that?" Belinda was losing patience.

"Maybe something associated with Thomas. Like his age or birth date."

Belinda considered this. "More likely it would be the date he was murdered. Try, what was it? Eleven-Seventy."

Hazel looked at her doubtingly. "Are you sure that's the date? We only have two more chances to get the password right."

"Yes, I'm sure," said Belinda crossing her fingers behind her back.

Hazel typed in 'S-A-M-O-H-T-1-1-7-0'. But they were doomed to disappointment. The password was refused.

"Now we only have one more go at it," said Hazel.

"I think we'd better wait until we see if Tommy or Peter know what it is."

Belinda sank down in a chair a picture of absolute despondency. She was sure the word was right. She sat upright.

"If the word Thomas is spelled backwards, try reversing the numbers as well."

Hazel looked at her.

"Are you sure you want to waste our last chance?"

Belinda nodded boldly.

"No worries," she said with a confidence she didn't really feel.

"Be it on your own head," said Hazel, as she very deliberately keyed in the password, 'S-A-M-O-H-T-0-7-1-1'.

The screen flickered and they gave a cry of delight as the file was opened. They crowded around the screen to read it.

The mystery of what happened to Becket's bones is a captivating legend. Some say at the King's command the bones were burnt; even more fanciful stories tell of them being fired from a cannon. There are also accounts claiming monks secured the bones before the destruction of the shrine and secreted them somewhere in the Cathedral.

As there is no solid evidence that the bones exist, I come to the question of what became of the Crown. It is safe to assume that the shrine in the Corona Tower, containing the Crown of St Thomas, that portion of his skull detached from his body when he was foully murdered, was destroyed along with the main shrine, but there is no mention of what happened to the section of St Thomas's skull it contained.

I must now take you back some thirty years or more when I was actively involved in an archaeological dig at the time of the removal of the 18th century façade at Bushmead Priory in Bedfordshire.

The façade was an ugly addition and it was a welcome relief when it was removed. But it afforded me the chance to undertake a dig and I acquired a collection of bones, both human and animal, along with household items from the 16th century and beyond.

These I catalogued and subsequently forgot. But recently when I began my research into the missing Crown I came across documents, which I will present later, that led me to believe that the monks had indeed spirited the Crown away from the Cathedral and out of the county, to be buried secretly at the Priory until such time, if ever, they could replace the relic in its proper place in Canterbury. That time never arose of course, as shortly after the Priory was sold into private hands.

This led me to re-examine the bones I had recovered during the dig, and to my great astonishment and delight I came to believe that I had in my possession the actual Crown of St Thomas.

Needless to say, I have treated it with the utmost respect and housed it in a fitting container until such time as I can reveal it to the religious community.

What followed was a lot of academic references to medieval documents that were believed to support the theory and conviction that the bone was the crown of the saint's head.

"So that's what it's all about," said Hazel fiddling with the keyboard before leaning back in her chair.

"And I'm willing to bet I know where it is," said Belinda.

It didn't take them long to reach the store room and open the Elizabethan chest. Carefully they began to remove the stored items, scrutinizing each in turn. It wasn't until they reached the bottom of the chest that they came upon a brown paper package tied with string. Carefully Belinda undid the string and folded back the paper. Before them was a small, flat gold box about six inches square and an inch in depth. It was locked.

"The small key," said Belinda, her voice tight with excitement.

Hazel fumbled in her pocket.

"Wait. It's in my bag."

She rushed off to the parlour. Belinda held the gilded box reverently in her hands. Could it really contain the relic of St Thomas?

Hazel returned breathless, the key held tightly in her fingers. It slid into the lock and Belinda turned it gently. With baited breath she lifted the lid.

An object about five inches in length and wrapped in a red silk square rested on a small piece of velvet. Reverently Belinda took it up and unfolded the silk covering.

Before them was a piece of bone. It was dark greyish-brown and stained with rusty blotches. The edges were broken and irregular. Both women stared at it for a moment in wonder and then at each other.

"Do you think it's real?" whispered Belinda, awed by the discovery.

"The Professor seemed to think so," said Hazel softly, for once almost lost for words.

Belinda looked again at the piece of bone.

"And we're the first people to see it in over four hundred years."

"Well, apart from the Professor," said Hazel meticulously.

Belinda folded the silk covering over the bone and locked the box.

"What shall we do with it?"

"If it's as valuable as people seem to think we'd be wise to keep it with us for the time being and keep quiet about it or at least until Miss Mowbray recovers and this whole mess can be sorted out. There are any number of goons anxious to get hold of it and who knows what they'll do if they know we have it. Plus if it is real, I imagine it actually belongs to the Cathedral."

They made their way back to the parlour, Belinda reverently carrying the gold box. At the door they froze. A man was sitting at the computer reading the file. He turned. It was Tommy.

Belinda slid the box behind her, out of sight.

"I see you're back from London." Her voice was cold.

"And I see you've cracked the file open," he said. "I congratulate you. So it was the Crown of St Thomas."

"You didn't know?" said Hazel.

"I suspected it."

"And you knew the password to open the file?"

"True. But I needed the USB file otherwise the password was useless."

"And you knew Miss Mowbray had it," said Belinda.

He looked at her. "Who else would have?"

"So you could have gone to the publishers, one in particular, Sir Justin, with the promise that if you could find the USB file you were in a position to deliver to him what he wanted, something that Miss Mowbray was refusing to give."

"Something like that," said Tommy smugly.

"A *lot* like that," said Belinda, "and for a high price, I imagine."

"You've got a good imagination," Tommy said, giving her a wink.

Hazel strode to the computer and switched off the power supply. The screen went blank. "You little snake." She reached for the USB. Tommy gave a derisive laugh and before she could reach it he quickly removed it from the computer and waved it at her.

"Now all I have to do is to find the Crown." He smiled and held the USB teasingly before Hazel. She grasped for it but he swiftly snatched it back out of her reach.

"Oooh, naughty Hazel wants what she can't have."

Hazel looked at him in silent rage. The telephone rang. Slowly backing away but keeping her eyes fixed on Tommy she picked up the receiver. "Hello … yes … I see … thank you for letting us know." She replaced the receiver and looked at Belinda. "That was the hospital. Miss Mowbray died half an hour ago."

Tommy gave a whimper and leapt to his feet, his face ashen, and his hands trembling. Without a word he rushed out into the orchard and clambered into a car. Belinda and Hazel watched him drive off.

"What's got into him?" said Hazel.

"Don't know, but he's got the file," Belinda replied.

"So have we," said Hazel. "I'd saved it to the hard drive after we read it. He's not the only smart one."

Belinda placed the box on the desk and sat down. "With Miss Mowbray gone, what should we do with this and the Professor's book?"

"We're just about finished the valuation so we can wrap up everything here. If her lawyer, Fosdyke, is true to his word, we'll get paid. I expect the best thing to do is to put everything else in the hands of the police."

"I suppose you're right. Will you take the relic?" She pushed the gold box to Hazel. "I'll finish up here. There's still that collection of odds and sods to be valued. I'll stay and do that. And I want to ring Mark. There's something we have to discuss."

She told Hazel all he had said about marriage to him and what it would mean. Hazel's eyebrows shot up in surprise.

"A title? Lady Muck. Darling, grab him with both hands and go galloping down the aisle. Offers like that don't come along every day."

Belinda smiled.

"I know, but I've decided to fly back to Melbourne once more to talk to Brad."

Hazel gave a sigh of frustration and gathered her things. "Granted, Brad's a sweet boy but you've kept Mark waiting for so long. Don't take his affection for you lightly. I'll see you back at the hotel and tomorrow we can go to the police and they can sort everything out with the solicitor."

With that she left.

Belinda began to climb the stairs to the Great Hall when she remembered she'd left her laptop in the parlour. She returned and to her annoyance saw that Hazel had forgotten to take the gold box. She picked it up along with her laptop and went upstairs to sort through the waiting items.

The day was ending and she switched on the desk lamp, a pool of light in the otherwise shadowy space, the gigantic hammerbeam roof above lost in the gloom. Belinda felt very small in the ancient room. She sat at the table and switched on the laptop. She placed the gold box near some of the items she was to evaluate. Bitter rain pitted itself against the windows and a strong howling wind blew up. The Manor House began to creak and groan

A 1930s sterling silver cigarette dispenser, a silver-plate art deco Ice Bucket and a 1920s Continental silver cigarette case with a sapphire clasp and an enamelled scene of a Bathing Belle were among the last remaining items that Belinda valued. She smiled at the Bathing Belle from long ago and estimated its worth at £2,000.

She was reaching for a Royal Doulton wall plaque when she heard footsteps on the stairs. Assuming it was Hazel she called, "Your memory's getting worse. You forgot the box." But there was no reply. A quiver of fear ran through Belinda as she realized she was alone in the house. She turned to the door. It opened slowly and Peter Jones stepped into the room.

Belinda gave a sigh of relief.

"Hello, Peter. You gave me a fright."

He closed the door and stood leaning back against it for a moment. Then he seemed to glide across the room, his enormous shadow created by the lamp increasing all the time. Suddenly he was at her shoulder. He put before her a framed drawing. The frame and glass were covered in dust and it was only after Belinda had wiped most of it off that she could see clearly what it was, an illustration of a stained glass window in a church.

"It's sixteenth century, from a church in Cheshire," said Peter in a low voice.

There were four figures representing the knights who murdered Thomas Becket at the altar in Canterbury Cathedral. They wore armour and held drawn swords. On ornamental scrolls were their names: William de Tracy, Richard le Breton, Reginald FitzUrse and Hugh de Moreville. A fifth figure in the centre bore the words, 'Martyrum Thomas'.

"Where did you find this?" asked Belinda.

"In the store room. Near the old chest." His voice had a curious flatness, which alarmed Belinda. "You know the one I mean. The one that's just been opened."

He picked up the cigarette case and examined it.

"Its good quality isn't it," said Belinda, feeling ill at ease at his nearness. "It should fetch a decent sum at auction."

Peter glanced at her and dropped the case into his pocket. Before Belinda could say a word he slid his hand smoothly, caressingly onto the back of her neck. She froze in fright.

"Did you kill Umm Walad?" he said huskily. His fingers increased their hold on her neck.

"I … I don't know what you mean," stuttered Belinda.

"She died, you know," said Peter, releasing his grip.

"Do you mean, Miss Mowbray?" said Belinda, now fully alarmed by his bizarre behaviour.

Peter seemed distracted and picked up some of the silver objects. He examined them in detail.

Belinda's eyes slid to the gold box containing the relic. While Peter was engrossed with the other items she reached out slowly and carefully slid the box behind the laptop and out of his sight.

Peter dropped the last of the silver items, drew in a deep breath and slowly looked around the vast room.

"She hid it, you know, St Thomas's Crown."

Belinda remained silent.

Peter moved away and began to look closely at the items displayed on the opposite wall. "She did it for me, but didn't tell me where she'd hidden it." He lingered near the display of rifles.

Her chest now tight with fear, Belinda reached over and slid the gold box off the table and down by her side, hoping that in the dark Peter wouldn't see what she was doing. Hazel's words that the relic belonged to the Cathedral came back to her and she wasn't about to hand it over to this madman.

Peter reached up and in a swift violent movement grasped one of the long pikes and wrenched it from the wall. He spun around and pointed the frightening weapon at Belinda.

Belinda, her heart pounding, edged her chair back preparing for a quick flight to safety.

Peter advanced slowly, the long thrusting spear getting closer and closer to her face until the sharp iron point was near her cheek.

"You and your friend have been searching through all the rooms here. I believe you've found it." His voice was guttural and his eyes filled with hate. "I *know* you've found it." He moved the pike slowly so that the iron tip caressed Belinda's cheek in a tormenting warning. "And by rights it's mine. So I want it. *Now.*"

Belinda carefully reached out with her free hand and took hold of the cigarette dispenser. "I think this is what you're looking for," she said in a thin, anxious voice.

She hurled it across the table towards Peter and at the same time, grasping the gold box, ran towards the door. But Peter had locked it.

Peter wasn't tricked by the silver dispenser and kicked it out of his path as he ran across the room after Belinda, holding the pike level before him.

Belinda struggled to turn the old iron key in the lock. She screamed in fright as the spearhead of the pike went smashing into the wooden door with a thunderous crash, a few inches from her head.

Peter struggled to free the pike. Belinda ran back into the room her mind racing, searching for a way of escape. Peter followed, both hands wildly swinging the long pike from side to side.

It was then he saw the gold box in Belinda's hand. His eyes lit up with fearsome intensity.

"I was right. You've got it." Once again he lunged at her, the pike passing by her ear. "Give it to me."

Terrified and mesmerised by Peter's transformation into a monster, Belinda backed away until she felt the cold stone of the giant fireplace between her shoulder blades.

With a terrifying cry like a marauding animal, Peter ran at full tilt across the room towards her. The pike was aimed at her heart. Belinda screamed. Her legs collapsed under her and she fell.

With a thud the iron spearhead of the pike struck the solid stone fireplace. Under the force at which it hit the rock-hard surface the ancient wooden shaft shattered on impact leaving a jagged edge, the reinforcing metal strips projecting like twin blades.

In that instant, Peter's fast moving body, propelled by his size and bulk, followed immediately, and the spiked edge of the shaft and the projecting metal plunged deep into his upper body.

With a cry of terror he staggered back, the head of the pike projecting from his chest. The remainder of the broken weapon fell from his hands and clattered to the floor as he clutched at the shaft imbedded in his body. His weakening fingers jerked ineffectually in a vain attempt to release it.

He fell to his knees blood rushing from his mouth.

He gave a gurgled utterance: "Umm Walad" and, as his eyes glazed over, fell back dead.

Belinda, choking back bitter bile, staggered to her feet and stumbled to the door. In a frantic desire to escape the scene of horror she fought to turn the key in the unyielding lock, shaking fingers unequal to the task. By drawing on every ounce of her remaining energy she forced the reluctant key, opened the door and half tumbled down the staircase and out, out into the now welcoming night and the cleansing rain. The gold box fell from her grasp and clattered down the front step. It split open on the stone path and the Crown, freed from its prison, slid unceremoniously into a muddy pool.

Chapter Eleven

The door of the cottage opened. Mrs Jones gazed at Belinda with forlorn eyes. It was late in the day and Belinda had had very little sleep. After Peter's attack on her and his subsequent death she had been with the police most of the time.

"You'd best come in." Mrs Jones stepped aside to allow Belinda to enter.

The room was small and cramped, without any distinguishing features. A worn sofa, odd chairs, some framed prints on the wall, an old television set, a cheap display cabinet filled to capacity with a higgledy-piggledy assortment of items and piles of old TV magazines stacked in a corner. An aged black and white cat lay asleep in front of an inefficient gas fire. A black and white film was playing on the TV. In another corner a sad plastic Christmas tree, with a smattering of baubles, the only colour in this monochrome room.

Mrs Jones turned the TV sound off leaving the actors to go through their actions mutely. She gestured towards a rickety chair.

"Sit yourself down."

Belinda did as she was bid. She still felt weak from the events of the past hours and was more or less operating on remote. Mrs Jones gathered the sleeping cat up and sat on the sofa with the animal on her lap. It barely woke, gave a raspy purr, and was soon asleep again. She patted its head in repetitive strokes but otherwise sat motionless staring blankly into space.

"Mrs Jones, I've given a statement to the police about what happened and I'm about to leave Canterbury, although the police will want to talk to me again so I expect I'll be back."

Mrs Jones seemed to be in another world.

She's in shock, thought Belinda. *Not surprising when her son had died so horribly.*

"The police have been asking me questions about Peter too, and told me that Muriel Mowbray was dead. Peter and her, both dead on the same day," said Mrs Jones slowly, her voice soft and distant. Her eyes wandered to the television set.

Belinda touched her arm.

"I wanted to see you before I left, to say how very sorry I am about Peter's death. You must be distraught."

Mrs Jones looked at the hand on her arm as though it was a foreign object and then looked up to Belinda as if she didn't understand the word 'distraught'. She merely nodded slowly.

"It must be dreadful losing your child," said Belinda, hoping in her clumsy way that she would be a comfort to the woman. "I can't imagine what you're going through but I want you to know …"

Mrs Jones interrupted. "He wasn't my child." Her soft voice was non-committal as though she was commenting on the weather or an obvious fact. She stroked the cat, which began to purr loudly. "No, he wasn't mine."

Belinda was bewildered. "Then whose?"

"I couldn't have a child, but I wanted one ever so much. Miss Mowbray was his mother."

Belinda was spellbound at this revelation as a thousand thoughts raced through her brain.

"So how did you come to care for Miss Mowbray's child? Did you adopt him?"

"Do you want your dinner?" said Mrs Jones, speaking to the cat as though Belinda didn't exist. The creature looked at her with a vacant stare. Mrs Jones said slowly in an impassive voice and addressing the cat: "Eventually, I did. You see Miss Mowbray fell pregn… I mean she was having a baby. The Professor was the father, but as he was about to be married, she couldn't tell him. Well, I mean she could have, but she didn't. So she went away, up north somewhere, to have the baby." Her voice faded away and there was a silence.

"And she came back to Canterbury afterwards," said Belinda, urging the woman to continue.

Mrs Jones turned her attention to Belinda.

"That's right. About a year or so later. She was going back to work with the Professor and as things had changed between them, she didn't want him to know he had a son, so she came to me and asked me to take care of the baby, I mean Peter, for her. She knew how I longed for a child. Of course I said yes. That's when my husband left me. He said he wouldn't have a little bastard in the house and wouldn't have anything to do with a child that wasn't his."

"So you raised Peter by yourself."

Mrs Jones spoke as though it was too much of an effort. "More or less. Miss Mowbray paid for everything and it meant that she could see him every day, but I always felt that she would eventually go and take Peter with her. That would have broken my heart, even though I knew he was a bit simple. Slow, you know?"

She was silent for a moment and then rose and walked quickly towards the kitchen. "Where are my manners? I didn't offer you a cup of tea."

Belinda put out her hand to stop her.

"Oh, please don't worry, Mrs Jones."

"No, no. I must give you tea, and a slice of Christmas cake." She disappeared into the kitchen.

It seemed clear to Belinda that the woman was confused but doing a routine thing like making the tea might prove beneficial to her, take her mind off the loss of her son. She could hear her clattering about in the kitchen and chatting to the cat, which had followed her, no doubt anticipating its dinner.

She called after her: "Mrs Jones. Peter sometimes used an expression. He used it again last night when …" She was about to say 'when he died' but bit her tongue. The woman didn't need to be reminded of his death. "He said something like, 'Um Wallan'."

Mrs Jones called back from the kitchen: "Oh, I'll tell you about that in a minute."

Belinda sat waiting and looked around the room. Its untidiness was oddly unsettling. Nearby she saw the carrier bag containing Miss Mowbray's diaries. Again she wondered why Mrs Jones had collected them. *Was it because she thought they might contain details of Peter's birth?* She rose and inspected the prints on the wall, but after brushing the dust off the glass could see they were of no value, except for one, which she recognised as an early Hogarth, one of his series of moral works, A Harlot's Progress. Belinda brushed more dust away and looked closer at the print. As she inspected it she became convinced it was an original probably dating from 1731. Did Mrs Jones know the value of the dusty print? Belinda smiled to herself. It had most likely been picked up in a flea market at some time. She was about to call to Mrs Jones and tell her that she had a valuable print hanging on her wall, when a sudden disturbing thought struck her. *Maybe Mrs Jones did know.*

Mrs Jones returned with the tea things on a tray.

"The tea's just drawing. Won't be long."

"So how did you manage to adopt Peter?" said Belinda.

Mrs Jones arranged the tea cups and cake.

"Oh that was easy, after I saw Miss Mowbray kill the Professor's wife."

For a moment Belinda thought she was hearing things.

"Did you say Miss Mowbray killed the Professor's wife?" she said in disbelief.

Mrs Jones looked surprised, as though it was common knowledge and an everyday event. Her manner changed and she became more animated.

"That's right. The night she pushed her down the stairs."

Belinda sat in her chair in shock.

"I don't believe it."

Mrs Jones looked hurt. She didn't want to be considered a liar and her voice gathered in strength.

"It's true I tell you. Saw it with my own eyes. It was late one night and the Prof and his wife were having a ding dong argument in the Great Hall. Peter was about two then and I'd gone over to let Miss Mowbray know that he'd developed croup, barking like a seal he was, and should I call the doctor.

"As soon as I entered the house I could hear their voices even down at the bottom of the stairs. I stood there listening for a while not sure what to do, when the door to the Hall opened and the Missus came out and yelled at the Prof, 'I want that woman out of the house by tomorrow. It's gone on long enough.' I stepped back so that she wouldn't see me when she came down.

"As she was about half way down, on the landing it was, Miss Mowbray came out from behind her where she'd been hiding, listening to the argument, and gave her such a shove. The Missus gave a shriek and tumbled down the stairs. She landed almost at my feet. Gave me such a turn, it did. But I got out quickly, didn't want to be seen there. Muriel knew that the Professor would inherit the house and she meant to get him to leave it to her.

"It was only afterwards that I began to think and so I went to Miss Mowbray and told her what I'd seen. I suggested that if I kept quiet and didn't tell the police what I knew, she should let me adopt Peter."

Belinda drew in a deep breath. Not only was she amazed at what Mrs Jones had said, but also at her almost serene attitude. Here she was describing a murder and blackmail and it was as though she was recounting events at a tea party.

"So Miss Mowbray agreed," said Belinda.

"She had no choice really," said Mrs Jones. "Of course I insisted that she continue to pay for Peter's upbringing and schooling and I never kept it a secret from him that she was his real mother."

"He knew that?"

"All his life. I think it's wrong not to tell a child."

"So his mother was a murderer?"

Mrs Jones nodded.

"In fact she was a murderer twice," said Belinda. "First there was the Professor's wife and then the Professor himself."

Mrs Jones raised her eyebrows as though the suggestion was a new idea for her to consider.

"The tea should be ready."

She returned to the kitchen.

Belinda, astounded at what she had just been told, glanced around the room. She rose, eager to leave. She doubted if she could swallow the proffered tea now. The display cabinet with its cluttered contents caught her eye. In the jumble of cups, plates and bric-a-brac rested some heavily tarnished silver bowls, spoons and jugs. Belinda picked one up. From what she could see the sterling hallmark showed it to be a London mark and probably around 1784. Another had a York hallmark and from her knowledge of silver she guessed it to be close to 1812. All the silver items bore similar hallmarks and Belinda knew their value. And more importantly, where they had come from. From the Manor House, along with the Hogarth print.

Belinda was about to close the glass door when she saw a wooden object half buried under the stored items. Carefully reaching in, she withdrew a heavy, roughly made club. The end had been drilled out and replaced with a lead weight, with rows of large hobnails hammered in and projecting around its edge. A leather strap designed to wrap around the user's wrist hung from the end. Belinda gaped at it in horror. Sticking to the nails were grey hairs and black, dried blood.

"It's not very polite to go through people's things." Mrs Jones's voice was judgmental. She stood at the door with the tea pot in her hand. She put it down and with an odd smile, took the club from Belinda's trembling fingers.

"Peter said we should get rid of it, but somehow I just couldn't. He didn't know I'd kept it."

Unnerved by Mrs Jones's manner Belinda instinctively backed away, a startling realization dawning on her.

"It was Peter," she said unsteadily, "not Miss Mowbray. *Peter* killed the Professor."

"Oh no, Peter would never do anything like that," Mrs Jones said in a voice full of disbelief.

But he had no hesitation in trying to kill me, thought Belinda, a point that Mrs Jones seemed prepared to overlook.

The woman sat on the sofa, the club beside her, chuckling away at the suggestion that her son was a murderer. The cat jumped onto her lap and let out a tiny squeak of contentment as she resumed patting it.

"Oh no, *he* didn't kill the Professor. That was me."

Belinda's eyes widened. She doubted if she could take any more disclosures.

"You?" she said weakly.

"Yes,' said Mrs Jones, almost as though she was describing a scene from one of her television soaps. "Miss Mowbray had just told Peter that the Professor was his father. She also told him how she had been cheated out of inheriting the Manor House, which she had intended to leave to Peter when she died.

"Peter also knew that the Professor, I suppose I should really say his father, had found something that involved a relic of St Thomas, a bit of old bone or something. I wanted his father to give it to him so that he could take it to that place at the Cathedral where they keep old things, the Archive it's called. He'd always wanted to work there since he was a teenager, but he wasn't smart enough they said. I thought if he could take the bone to them they would give him a job. That's what he wanted most in the world and I thought it was the least a father could do for his son."

"And the Professor wouldn't give it to him," said Belinda.

"That's right. Miss Mowbray and I both went to see the Professor, and Muriel told him that Peter should have it as he was his son. But that evil man would have none of it. Said he had no son. Called Muriel a liar and all sorts of names, which upset her no end, then laughed at her for being in love with him over the years and said it amused him. And then he turned on me and said that he'd die first before giving the relic, as he called it, to Peter who he thought was crazy."

"So you killed him."

Mrs Jones gave a sudden grin.

"Bashed his head in with this wooden club. He had plenty of them scattered about the house." She gave an excited chuckle at the memory, picked up the club and as though mesmerised with it, turned it around and back and forth. "Muriel said 'good riddance' or something like that, and went and made sure the door was locked. Said as she couldn't get the house to leave to Peter she could get the bone for him.

"She said it might be worth a lot of money and I was to let her handle everything, and so she paid the doctor and the undertaker good money, far too much in my opinion, to keep it secret. Muriel told them of her idea, actually it was the Professor's idea but she used it, to build a shrine for the relic and she would make a lot of money from tourists. She offered to make them partners if they did what she asked, and so they fixed up the death certificate. Had him cremated the next day so there couldn't be any enquiry. We both didn't want her son – my son, as well – to be left with nothing. He was her Rock, you know."

Belinda looked at her blankly.

"She called him her Rock. You know? From the Bible, 'You are Peter, and upon this rock …? He was all she had." She looked down at the murder weapon. "He was all I had too," she added softly.

Both the women were silent for a moment, Belinda trying to absorb all she'd just heard; Mrs Jones pondering the future. She looked despondently at Belinda.

"I didn't tell the police."

Belinda, still recovering from the revelations, gave a faint gasp.

"I'm afraid you must, Mrs Jones." She didn't add that she herself would have to report to the police all that she'd been told.

Mrs Jones gave her a searching look and frowned.

"Yes, I suppose you're right. At least Peter is beyond any more hurt."

Belinda shivered at the thought that the murder weapon had been there all the time she was in the room and was again in the hands of a murderer. She hurriedly moved to the front door, wanting to get away from this mad woman.

"I must go. I'll let myself out."

At the door she struggled with the lock.

Mrs Jones dropped the cat on the floor and edged out of her seat.

"Would you like to look at it again?" she said in a conspiratorial whisper, following Belinda to the door.

"At what?' said Belinda fearfully.

Mrs Jones held up the hideous club.

"The Professor once told me it was used during World War One for raiding the trenches at night. It was called a 'quiet weapon', he said, an easy way of killing the enemy. A quick blow and ..."

With her frail arms she swung the club in an arc above her head. She gave a baleful smile and moved closer to Belinda, the frightening club swinging from her wrist.

"Oh, I forgot. You asked about Umm Walad didn't you. You wanted to know what it means. Well, I'll tell you while I pour the tea."

Chapter Twelve

In the evening light Belinda sank back into the comfortable leather seat in Hazel's Mercedes as it made its way up St Dunstan's Street, away from Canterbury and towards Bath. Hazel had picked her up at the police station where she'd told the police everything Mrs Jones had revealed. As she'd left, the police were on their way to speak to the woman.

Hazel took her eyes off the road for a moment to look at her friend. She was pale and looked exhausted.

"Are you all right?" she asked with concern.

Belinda gave a weak smile.

"As well as can be expected after being attacked by a madman and watching him being skewered to death. And then finding out our lunch lady is a murderer."

"When we get home I'm taking you straight to the doctor," said Hazel. "You're in shock if you ask me".

"Good idea. When this is all over I want to be OK to fly home to Melbourne."

"You're still going ahead with that idea?"

Belinda sighed.

"I've decided to marry Mark."

"Not a moment too soon," said Hazel with a mocking smile.

"Let me finish," said Belinda. "When I marry things will be different."

"Yes, you'll be Lady Muck for one thing."

Belinda ignored her jibe; she knew Hazel was a snob and having a 'Lady' for a friend would please her no end. "I'll be marrying into a well established English family. Me? I'm just a girl from Melbourne. They have money, a title, a country house and all that goes with that life style. Plus a mother-in-law who doesn't think I'm good enough for her son, but no doubt I'll be expected to produce a son and heir."

"Is that a bad thing?"

Belinda smiled and shook her head.

"Just once before it all happens, I want to go home just as myself, as I am."

"And see your boyfriend, Brad," said Hazel amiably.

"My ex-boyfriend. Yes, I'll see him and I think I should tell him face to face that I'm marrying Mark. Not on the phone or by email. He deserves better than that."

They drove past St Dunstan's Church and Belinda recalled the excitement she had felt on her arrival in the ancient city. Now she couldn't wait to get away from it.

"So that's how Miss Mowbray got hold of the file," said Hazel, changing the subject prudently.

"Yes. She'd been working with the Professor and knew what he'd discovered. When Mrs Jones murdered him she took the USB and hid it along with the Crown to sell the book to the highest bidder and build a shrine for the relic. She was looking after her son. It and the book would make a lot of money for them both she believed. Funnily enough, his adoptive mother wanted much the same thing for Peter. The Crown would get him a position in the Archives, or so she thought."

"And what about the Crown that all the fuss was about?"

"The people from the Archives have had a quick look at the bone and are doubtful. There'll have to be a series of tests on it and that won't happen until the police release it. They're also checking the documents the Professor offered as evidence that the bone was really St Thomas's. They have their doubts about them as well."

"I have some further news," said Hazel.

Belinda wondered if she could take in any more.

"Oh, really?" There was no enthusiasm in her voice.

"It seems that after he heard Miss Mowbray had died, Sir Justin had a fit of the guilts and confessed to the police that he had hired Tommy to rough Miss Mowbray up a little to convince her she should allow him to publish the book. Seems that Tommy got carried away and overdid it. Now, of course, he will be charged with murder or manslaughter or something."

"Have they caught him?"

"Got him at Heathrow as he was about to board a flight to Los Angeles."

Belinda was silent. She wanted to forget the whole episode and just get home to Melbourne.

"Can you believe that little sparrow, Mrs Jones?" Hazel laughed. "Butter wouldn't melt in her mouth and here she is a blackmailer and a murderer." She shook her head in disbelief. "I suppose she'll be found insane. And that weird son, or adopted son. She was just as weird as him. What was that expression he used 'Oh wally', or something like that."

Belinda slumped further in her seat as the warmth in the car and the hum of the engine made her drowsy.

"Oh, I can tell you about that."

She slipped into a doze.

"Well, tell me about it," snapped Hazel loudly.

Belinda came to with a start.

"Oh yes. It was Umm Walad. That's what he said."

She began to drift off again.

"Wake up, woman," said Hazel irritably.

"Mmmm… it was something that Peter found in some medieval books he'd been studying. Umm Walad. And he called his mother, I mean Miss Mowbray, that."

"Why?" asked Hazel tightly. *Really, it was like pulling teeth.*

"It was a medieval expression meaning, 'mother of a child'."

"And?" said Hazel, wanting more details.

But Belinda was asleep.

The End

For more books in the Belinda Lawrence Mystery series, please visit
www.vividpublishing.com.au/briankavanagh

PUBLISHING

CPSIA information can be obtained at www.ICGtesting.com
Printed in the USA
LVOW11s1545140915

454091LV00001B/57/P